A Wilderness
of Mirrors

By the same author
Snow Moon
After Blossom Viewing
Pillars of Fire
Gingko Leaves
Chrysanthemum Garden
Interiors
The Distances
Leaves and Angels
Ekphrasis
River Mist
Invisible Rivers
The Sound of Purple
The Distances of Sleep
City of Shaded Light
Heart Murmurs
Letters to My Parents

A Wilderness of Mirrors

Steven Carter

Alba Publishing

Published by Alba Publishing,
P O Box 266, Uxbridge
UB9 5NX, United Kingdom
www.albapublishing.com

© 2014 Steven Carter
All rights reserved
No part of this publication may be reproduced, stored in a retrieval system, or transmitted by any form or by any means electronic, mechanical, photocopying, recording or otherwise without the prior written permission of the copyright owners.

A catalogue record for this book is available from the British Library

ISBN: 978-1-910185-06-3

Edited, designed and typeset by Kim Richardson
Cover picture © Eugenesergeev/Dreamstime.com
Printed and bound by Bookpress.eu

10 9 8 7 6 5 4 3 2 1

Acknowledgements

The following haibun originally appeared in the following journals: "The Cemetery" in *Kokako;* "Out, out" and "Song for Edmund" in *Contemporary Haibun Online;* "Two Dreams of Annie" in *Haibun Today.* "Equinox" originally appeared in *Ripples,* published by Red Moon Press.

Contents

Book I
–Twelve-acres I　　　　7
–Twelve-acres II　　　59

Book II
– Steven/Peter　　　　75

Book III
– Hic et Ille　　　　139

We are, I know not how, double in ourselves, so that what we believe we disbelieve, and cannot rid ourselves of what we condemn.
—Montaigne

Try as he might, he could not get his face out of the mirror; to his great exasperation, he always blocked his own view. Of course deep down he knew that the transparencies he sought were not in the mirror at all, but to look anywhere else would by then have been inconceivable.
—Don Paterson

Book I

Twelve-acres

I

I Too Am In Arcadia

"I was in Paradise this afternoon."

That was my cue to head for my room, sit on the bed and tumble into deep depression.

My mother, who'd seen me in this mood before, knew better than to resume her ringing endorsement of Twelve-acres.

Twelve-acres: a Christian Science group home in Los Altos—the town where I'd spent a year in another foster home three years earlier.

On our way to the home from Palo Alto—a family friend was driving us; mom didn't own a car—tears sprang to my eyes and my braver younger brother laughed at me.

We were welcomed at the boys' dorm by Mrs. Slack, the assistant director. Genuine, kind, ebullient, she took us under her wing, showing off the premises and staying with us as we met the other kids and unpacked in the rooms assigned by age.

In the early going at Twelve-acres Mrs. Slack—unlike the more aloof director Mrs. Sloane—became an anchor for me, easing the pain of relocation to another venue and another school.

I'd begun to think of her as a second mother, Eve for my mother's Paradise regained—when she disappeared.

I asked our housemother where she was; she didn't know or wouldn't say.

I asked several others—no one said anything.

Only weeks later, when her name came up in a conversation between two housemothers, did I learn that Mrs. Slack had been busted for embezzlement from Twelve-acres and was awaiting trial.

>Wings folding in the breeze—
>Dying butterfly

The cemetery

It's a stretch, but I could've ridden my bike from Twelve-acres to Saratoga, where my father is buried.

Lying abed in the dorm, watching rain shimmer the window, I sometimes thought of doing so—just taking off, whizzing through the gate, heading south on San Antonio Road which ran from Los Altos down to San Jose.

But what would I do when I got there? I didn't even know where his grave was (fifteen years after he died my mother would join him).

Cemeteries fascinate me—blossoms and shadows of cherry trees, some a century old; worn gravestones leaning slightly toward each other as if exchanging confidences:

"They say don't speak ill of the dead," one says.

"Why not?" replies another. "What do they think we say about the living?"

My paternal grandmother Cora was still alive then, living in the Saratoga house my father built for her back in the thirties; but I had no wish to pay a visit—pay being the key word, because I knew that seeing her would cost more disillusionment beyond what I'd already experienced. She didn't come once to visit my brother and me at Twelve-acres.

Years later, after my mother's death, I did visit the Saratoga cemetery. Later still, I wrote:

At my parents' graves in Saratoga I feel the presence of something so much larger than I that, incongruously, the word ridiculous pops into my head. It awakens the decades-old memory of witnessing my mother's death; this time, however, it's something else that I'm experiencing. Well, if not death,

then what?
Then I have it.
The something brings me to my knees in the tall grass, leaning forward. I have to—have to—touch the names cut into dark gray stone.

      Graves
          All the lives in mine

Indian summer's Indian summer

Twelve-year-olds rarely think of suicide, but the prospect clouded my mind once or twice: particularly when time's tick-tocks seemed maddeningly slow.

Years later, when I remembered these dark moments at Twelve-acres, the following occurred to me:

Suppose human beings were born with a self-destruct button where our noses are.

Then suppose at the age of eighteen DNA kicked in and we were "required" to press the button.

The race would still continue—richer, however, for the eternal hours of (relative) innocence we'd inherit. (Or vice-versa!).

—When human life-expectancy was much lower than now: no high-tech, no nuclear weapons, no mass annihilation. Strife, yes; killing, yes: but none of the above.

As Don Paterson writes, "What fools we were to sign up to time."

> Shaping all
> But the wind,
> The wind

Passages

Usually we rode the bus to and from school: Covington Junior High was in town, Twelve-acres in a rural area of Los Altos. On the first day of classes, though, for some reason I distrusted the bus and rode my bike the four miles.

That cool, overcast day in 1955 was terrifying to me—like all kids I hated playing musical schools not to say musical homes, foster or otherwise. When I got to school I huddled next to the door of my home room, trying not to cry and bitterly ashamed for feeling the way I did.

A tall woman approached me; I recognized her from three years before, when I'd been in the other foster home in Los Altos—Mrs. Whitten, my fourth-grader teacher at Hill-View School.

Smiling, she said, "Hello again, Steven! Still doing the good work?"

Blinking tears from my eyes, I said I hoped I was.

. . . Soon enough, however, I was sent to the vice-principal Mr. Major who, not unkindly, suggested that I mend my ways. I did not.

I felt on the periphery of things, a star without a galaxy, adrift in space but not in time—I was too adept a classroom clock-watcher for that!

Still, I grew to like Covington eventually, even winning an essay contest on dental health; my prize was a Parker pen, which I promptly lost.

. . . At Twelve-acres dreams at night were of my early childhood home in Alto—not to be confused with Palo Alto—and a willow tree which grew in our back yard. More than half a century on, in my late sixties, I wrote:

Talismanic, the willow tree keeps its heart hidden from me, but I know some of its secrets. One day, equipped with a hammer, boards, and nails clenched between my teeth, I climb the thick, gnarled trunk to build a crude tree house, just long enough to lie down in.

Other days I scamper like a monkey from room to room of the tree's green mansions—for it is a house of many mansions—and spy on next-door Sheila, a fourth-grade classmate riding her pony around the small corral her father built in her back yard.

Sometimes at night the tree sings to me, its harp of leaves and branches accompanied by wind-storms off San Francisco Bay. But what's most deeply rooted in my memory is simply gazing at those branches, a dozen shades of green, tumbling almost to the ground, reminding me always of girls washing their hair by a stream and then, on hands and knees, tossing it forward to dry in the warm sun, so that their faces are hidden.

                Center of the universe—
                        Turning and turning
                              Eyes on a friendly star

Halloween

An adult, I forget who, built a bonfire in an open area near the gate and, adorned in costumes—I was a pirate—we brought bags of marshmallows, graham crackers and chocolate provided by the housemothers.

My eccentric friend Roger from Palo Alto came in costume. His parents joined the group.

I was certainly happy to see Roger; beyond that, happy that an obligatory full moon had joined the party. It was one of those rare moments in my life when I actually felt euphoric; as always, I couldn't pin down precisely why.

After roasting marshmallows and wolfing down s'mores, we went trick or treating in the small neighborhood abutting Pine Lane. I know now that my euphoria stemmed from the fact that I was wearing a costume, therefore becoming "someone else"; the feeling would repeat itself a few weeks later, during the Christmas play.

This is as it should be, a voice whispered in my ear. Yes, many of us felt abandoned and betrayed by our parents; but for this wink of eternity wearing its own All Hallows Eve costume, planets and stars were lined up the right way.

Back in the dorms we dove into our sacks of goodies. After chomping a Snickers bar, my favorite candy, I opened a napkin configured into a bag, tied with an orange ribbon. The housemother said kindly,

"That should be all for now, Steve. Save the rest; you don't want to get sick to your stomach!"

I undid the bow, reached in the bag, and brought out a handful of desiccated dog turds.

Lost moon
Chasing what chases me
In dreams

Carcassonne

I arrived at Twelve-acres in early September. By mid-November I was kicked out.

I overheard Mrs. Sloane say, "He's too angry and unpredictable."

A Christian Science practitioner named Clem Collins took my side, convincing the director to give me another chance. I could've strangled him.

—One evening in December, walking back to my bedroom from the communal bathroom of the boys' dorm, I heard sobbing.

The housemother's door was open; I saw her sitting on the bed, head in hands. I was afraid to intrude, but something told me to go in. —What can a twelve-year-old say to an adult crying in his presence?

I put a hand on her shoulder:

"What's the matter, Mrs. Davidson?"

She looked up at me, eyes shining. "It's just that—"

She looked down again.

"Is it . . . this?" I ventured; "this" being the boys' dorm which could get pretty rowdy. A few days ago I'd had a fistfight with another kid from up the hall.

She nodded, resting her hands in her lap.

"It's getting too much for me," she said, wiping her eyes.

"Maybe if we promised—" I began lamely, then trailed off.

Again she looked up at me, smiling for the first time.

". . . You're very kind," she said, then started crying again. "Maybe one day you'll be President of the United States."

Less than a week later, Mrs. Davidson was gone, to be temporarily replaced with a Mr. Little, whom I also liked. But then, very early one morning, in the middle of my happy dream about escaping into the night, he came in the room and shook me violently; I can't remember why.

Not knowing who it was, and still half-asleep, I took a swing, just missing him.

>Sixty years on—
>>Same me (or not)

Pink Horse Ranch

By age twelve I'd learned the old secret: If you're going through a rough patch, try to remember a time when things were worse, and then you'll feel better. (The opposite is also true, but that didn't occur to my nascent sensibility).

And so, in the early going at Twelve-acres, I "entertained" myself by recalling snippets of life at my first foster home in Los Altos—a few miles away on Moody Road up in the hills:

. . . Verbal (and sometimes physical) abuse was Kate's specialty. This became apparent to me the first or second day after I arrived at her small group home: I walked in on her screaming at a six-year-old boy for some minor offense.

And yet, because I felt invisible in my new surroundings, I needed somehow to establish an identity as authentic as the one I left behind. The only way to do so was to be recognized by Kate, my surrogate mother. She liked to spend Saturdays with her cronies at a small but luxurious resort a few miles down Moody Road from the home. Occasionally she took us kids along, which wasn't a bad thing: we'd swim and horseback ride while Kate sipped drinks topped with tiny paper umbrellas and chatted with her Junior League friends around the pool.

One warm afternoon it occurred to me that here was a chance to be recognized not only by Kate but by the other ladies as well. So I climbed out of the pool and walked over to them. Something in my mind shouted a shrill warning because by then I'd seen Kate in action many times, and I knew full well what was probably going to happen.

Trembling a little, I hesitated, and yet an irresistible urge kept pushing me toward the women sitting under a huge yellow- and white-striped umbrella. My impression was of red finger- and toe-nails, clicking bracelets, tinkling ice cubes, the crossing and uncrossing of tanned legs.

When I reached the group of chattering women, I stood dumbly in front of Kate. My lips parted, but I found I had nothing to say. Kate shifted in her chair and looked at me over the rims of her deep purple sunglasses. Then she put her drink down.

"What are *you* standing there like a simpleton for?" she demanded. "God, you're pathetic. Isn't he pathetic?" she asked a friend who said nothing.

Then to me: "Get back in the pool with the others!"

I quickly obeyed. Was the unpleasantness worth it? Yes and no. Kate might simply have ignored me, which would've been worse, I know now, than being yelled at.

       Shimmering—
          Eyes wide open
              Underwater

Let's make a deal

God is dead.
    Nietzsche

Once upon a time, the gods (pick a god, any god) invented a universe.
At the same time they invented cosmic blackmail.
—I dabbled in it myself at Twelve-acres, demanding of Clem Collins in so many words:
What self-respecting deity would whisk me from home and school in Palo Alto and, like Dorothy in Oz, plop me down, anxious and frightened, in a strange land?
. . . Years later, when I taught World Lit to university sophomores, I lectured on how the saintly Alexei in *The Brothers Karamazov* becomes a cosmic blackmailer.
Disillusioned that the body of a beloved monk stinks after he dies, Alexei threatens the Supreme Being with disbelief if He doesn't change the rules of nature and take away the odor.
There are untold thousands who junked their faith in a benevolent Creator because the skies didn't darken over Auschwitz. *I simply can't see believing in a God who allows—*
Problem: Let's say God darkens the skies. Then what? Like all blackmailers, you up the ante. *Strike Hitler dead so the killing will stop.* He does that. *Feed the starving in Africa.* He does that. Eventually things get personal: *See to it that my friends succeed (or fail).*
. . . Then, really personal: *Fill up my bank account and keep on filling it. While you're at it, deliver a brand new Mercedes to my front door.*

You see where this is going. Once He's granted your every wish, the universe is re-invented in your image and likeness. Congrats! You've become God—the deity you despise and have contempt for.

And you remember: the only way to stop a committed blackmailer is to kill him—the farthest thing from my mind, needless to say, at the age of twelve.

Poor Clem Collins! He could never convince me that I was barking up the wrong anti-doctrine.

Gardens

Are earthly gardens attempts to resurrect the Garden; even as we resurrect Jesus on Easter?

—A return from exile? —Or, as the witch's mirror of my brain would have it, a return to exile?

I began to wonder vaguely about such things when I attended Christian Science Sunday school at Twelve-acres. These fledgling thoughts came to me when I was on "garden duty"—weeding and pruning flowers and shrubs.

(Much later, this mature notion: *Can the distance between Eden and Gethsemane be measured?*)

—And: Are gardens smug reminders that we, too, are Creators, happily bereft of the boring skies of eternal clouds; ripe fruit that never fall; sparkling streams running with water not booze (remember the song The Big Rock Candy Mountain?).

This just in: Eve ate the apple not out of disobedience, but because she and her boyfriend were bored to tears.

—Tears in Paradise?

I was in Paradise this afternoon.

Long ago, sixteen years after Twelve-acres, I met a guy who specialized in cultivating winter gardens.

He lived in Portland, Oregon, whose climate is ideal for such endeavors. I see him in my mind's eye, a mysterious dark figure in a Chinese print of mist and pine trees.

When I asked why he went to the trouble—Portland has more than its share of farmer's markets—he said,

"It gives me something to do; Portland can be pretty boring in the winter."

Veiled
 By morning mist,
  Morning mist

OTHER VOICES, OTHER—

That year winter came in like a pride of lions and hung around into early spring.

In Northern California the Eel, American, Napa, and Sacramento rivers flooded; there was high water in some areas surrounding Twelve-acres.

I remember trees being thrashed by the wind like rag dolls shaken by a dog.

And I loved it—loved the sound of wind in the trees and rain lashing my window in the dorm. —So much so that one sleepless night I decided to sneak out. Bundling up as best I could, I crawled through the window onto the walkway in front of the dorm, welcomed by the open arms of darkness and cold.

Where have you been, Steven? We've been expecting you.

Hunching a yellow raincoat around my shoulders, I explored the grounds of Twelve-acres, so different at night. I walked to the big front gate, pushed it open—it was never locked—turned and looked upward where the wooden sign TWELVE-ACRES used to be (I'd smashed it with a rock the week before).

Crossing fields of oak and pine trees and flowers curled up for the night, I was acutely aware of the presence of mountains not far away, though I couldn't see them. I knew these fields like the back of my hand, even in the dark, so there was no danger of getting lost.

Why not keep walking to the edge of the world? What might I encounter along the way? —Perhaps the mountain lion I dreamt about the night before.

It's about time, kid, he hisses at me. . .

I picked up a small stone and tossed it upward into the dark, catching it once, twice, three times before it disappeared in the wet grass.

The moon broke through a bank of clouds, illuminating the trees around me; the rain thinned, the wind died, and I plopped down under a live-oak to rest.

Then, as the sky turned gray and I heard the chug-chug of a garbage truck on Pine Lane, I made my way back to the home—disgruntled since there was never any danger of getting lost.

    Pinks of dawn
        Catching the light
            A red-tailed hawk

Out, out—

1

Sometime around the holidays I began a love affair with the Sargasso Sea.

On a bookshelf below the TV in the boys' dorm, an *Encyclopedia Britannica* had been gathering dust and dead moths for who knows how long. I'd always been interested in the Sea—interested in all things bizarre—so one weekend morning I hauled the S volume back to my room and began to read.

(Many years later, I also fell for Ezra Pound's extended Sargasso Sea metaphor in *Portrait of a Woman*—the poem beginning, "Your mind and you are our Sargasso Sea.")

The Sea is an extraordinary deep blue and super-clear, even with all that flotsam and jetsam (it's also an eel breeding ground); I was surprised, too, at how big the thing is, taking up a fourth of the Atlantic.

What fascinated me in particular—of course!—were the untruths associated with the Sea—shipwrecks, sea serpents, even ancestors of the Loch Ness Monster.

But Father Ezra was right: long before I discovered his work, I was my own Sargasso Sea—and, if I wanted to be honest with myself (usually not the case), I was OK with that.

Father Ezra:
> *In the slow float of differing light and deep,*
> *No! There is nothing! In the whole and all*
> *—Nothing that's quite your own.*
> *Yet this is you.*

—Which is to say, No One.

2

Christmas we foster kids put on a play for the parents in the "Big House," a rich family's residence back in the day.

I forget what the play was or which role I had, but I remember the rehearsals and the performance as some of the happiest days of my life.

Why?

—We performed on a broad landing beneath the winding stairs to the upper floors, and sat in the darkness awaiting our turn to go on. This was terrific, because it allowed me to exchange kisses with a girl unseen by housemothers and Mrs. Sloane, who directed the play.

When I went onstage, feelings of bliss washed over me: suddenly I was someone else, whisked to a voluptuous dimension featuring neither past nor present.

It doesn't matter that I can't remember my role, since *au fond* I was No One—strutting for ten minutes back and forth on stage, half-aware of smiles and nods in the audience and fully aware of the darkness beyond the tall, beveled living room windows. (I avoided stage fright by speaking my lines to the darkness not the audience.)

Everyone commented on my excellent performance.

      Pale moon—pale
      Face in the window
           Ghost of my father

3

Bamboo forest

That's what we called it—an extensive stand of bamboo growing beyond the north end of the girls' dorm.

We scrambled down a hill to where the bamboo was thickest and commenced to smooch and hug as the housemothers did their thing: out of sight and out of mind.

Thud! Cupid fired his rubber-tipped arrows again and again as we tried to lose ourselves in each other, sometimes successfully, sometimes not. Light-years from what the French call the little death, or the orgasm, we were satisfied to explore the lowlands of Eros.

We closed our eyes, bumping chins and noses before finding each other's lips.

In the darkness, unknowingly—unconsciously, I mean—we did the innocent math: 1+1 = 0.

> Before the fall the fall
>   Of a shy glance

1 CONTACT

"Are you happy?"
—Always the wrong question.
"Who's happy?"
—Always the correct answer.
. . . Or so I thought in my early twenties.

I must've felt that way ten years earlier at Twelve-acres, but the words didn't find me.

No problem. They were "found" by these two unfamiliar voices I heard around a corner of the Big House. I was pulling weeds in the garden and by the time I looked, the speakers were gone.

I never learned who they were.

So what? Thinking about the mysteries of life was a bittersweet pleasure which, in my fevered imagination, became tangled up in the adult conversations I overheard at Twelve-acres.

Six years later, at UC Berkeley, I dropped Christian Science like a hot potato on realizing that it inveighed against drinking, smoking, and pre-marital sex.

—And yet CS gave me a lifelong belief in what Emerson called the NOT ME—the Mystery outside myself which, at Twelve-acres, and in an egoistic young punk like myself, was a lifesaver.

For me the NOT ME evolved into a kind of anti-faith: things happened or didn't happen because—

—Because, to my bent sensibility, they were written in a leather-bound volume entitled:

Nothing is written.

Field of nightmares
   Glints
      Of hidden water

Night Journey

Everyone had rotating jobs at Twelve-acres—this week in early February I drew kitchen duty. Fine with me: I liked the cooks Mr. and Mrs. Porterfield, liked their back-and-forth as they prepared the meals.

"Why doesn't he ever write?" Mrs. Porterfield asked her husband as they prepared supper. "He," I gathered, was their prodigal son.

I missed most of the reply, catching only the word "—busy."

These privileged glimpses into adult lives fascinated me. I was—I won't say obsessed, but certain deeply curious—about the bifurcation point between adolescence and adulthood. Naturally I figured it was a gradual process, but who knew? Maybe it could happen overnight.

With me it did.

One Friday night Mr. Porterfield drove three or four of us up to the San Francisco Cow Palace to watch an NBA basketball game: Celtics vs. Warriors. (That was the great Celtic team featuring rookies Bill Russell, K.C. Jones and a star-studded cast of vets.)

It happened on the way home on Highway 101.

A young female "chaperone" (May she live forever in the Eros Hall of Fame!) whispered in my ear:

"Do you and Sharon want to go back there?"—*there* being the spacious empty space between the second row of seats and the tailgate. Up till a few days earlier, Sharon's and my relationship was Platonic; then things began to change.

—The other kids were asleep and the station wagon was too dark for Mr. Porterfield to notice. We crawled over the back seat, grabbed a blanket, and bundled up just shy of the tailgate as raindrops spattered the rear window.

We made out, as the saying goes—goes nowhere, it turned out, since we were too shy to push the envelope too far.

No matter: in the rain-shadows her beauty alone would've sufficed. Decades later I'd return to those moments in the rickety station wagon when I recalled Paul Verlaine's *I hear the little sound of it raining in my heart.*

I said "I love you" for the first time in my life. She reciprocated.

Next day the roof caved in. At lunch Sharon ignored me, simply looking the other way when I said something to her. She didn't seem angry; that would've been too easy.

She was—indifferent. And that was that.

I never knew what the deal was. Pride—twelve-year-old pride!—prevented me from asking Sharon anything further; I simply walked away from her walking away from me.

—And nursed my suffering as one day I would nurse and be nursed by glasses of Chardonnay.

Not surprisingly I was sure I'd personally discovered all the clichés about females I would learn to articulate later on in life—fickle, mysterious, *What do women want,* etc., etc.

A zillion years later, on a cloudy afternoon when my thoughts again drifted back to Sharon, the following came to me (it takes place in Paris):

—A sky of mother-of-pearl.
Pink cobwebs of vapor trails, under-lit by the morning sun: Mirage fighter jets on maneuver, their mission being to protect themselves from government budget cuts.

In the Luxembourg Gardens, a group of small boys sail paper boats in a fountain. A few yards away three little girls sit on a bench slurping *glâce au chocolat* while their mothers chat.

Suddenly a squabble breaks out and one boy sinks the boat of another, whereupon both boys burst into tears. Observing this the three girls begin giggling.

"Why do they find that so funny?" an onlooker asks his companion.

"Actually, they're learning a valuable lesson," the other replies, folding up his *International Herald-Tribune*. "They're starting to appreciate how different they are from boys, even at an early age."

"And when they grow up?"

"The difference between them will be this: when the boys say 'I love you' in the heat of passion, they'll regret it more. When the girls say 'I hate you' in the heat of passion, they'll regret it less."

               Spine broken—
               Under a bench
                    A *Collected Plato*

Equinox

The saving grace of Twelve-acres was an abundance of young females—at least two girls to every boy.

. . . Boys and girls together, quivering on the horizon of adolescence, washed up on an island of oak trees, golden poppies, yellow fennel, and lupine, with nothing to do after coming home from school but develop crushes on each other and perform innocent experiments with sex under the trees: out of sight of the housemothers and Mr. Rice the slovenly caretaker.

Thanks to the epic winter, that spring the Los Altos hills were usually bright green. The week of spring break the dorms emptied as kids went home to spend Easter with their families. Just two of us remained: the thirteen-year-old Mary Ann and I.

I was disappointed and disgruntled, not because I couldn't go home, but because my girlfriend Annie would be gone for ten days (the pain of Sharon's rejection had eased with time).

I barely noticed Mary Ann, who'd arrived at the foster home after the first of the year (like me, she moved from school to school; Covington was her fifth school and my sixth). She was "homely as a mud fence," as I overheard one housemother remark to another when she thought nobody was listening.

I certainly had no time for Mary Ann. For her part Annie took perverse delight in making her life miserable. "You have your own secrets!" Annie snarled ambiguously at her one day, reducing Mary Ann to tears. She had a crush on me, which may have provoked Annie's remark and the ongoing wrangle between jealous twelve-year-olds.

One day during the break I was shooting hoops on the recreation hall's small playground when Mary Ann suddenly appeared, playfully stole the ball from me and sank a fifteen-footer. I tossed the ball to her, daring her to repeat the feat, which she did three times in a row. I could afford to be kind to her because Annie wasn't around. That cowardly knowledge may have been the first flash of real guilt I'd experienced.

We shot hoops, she laughing and teasing me even as I kept longing for Annie and Sharon. Then, three or four days into the vacation, Mary Ann started to look good to me. At first I resisted it—thoughts of her dun-colored hair, protruding lower lip, and freckles kept washing over me like cold water. But we continued to meet on the basketball court and take long walks around the twelve acre grounds of the home, spending hours together with no one else to talk to.

I knew she was in love with me—telling myself smugly and shamefully that she'd be a lead-pipe cinch, were I so inclined. Then, one gorgeous California afternoon of high clouds, bright blue skies, and wildflowers curtseying among the live-oaks, I was so inclined.

And she rebuffed me. She shook her head—mournfully, I remember thinking. I'll never forget the look on her face—it seems to me now as complex an expression as any twelve-year-old could muster. Bitterness, sadness, regret, all mixed with a kind of knowingness reflected in her small smile and a slight downturn of the eyes—she picked a lupine, twirling it once or twice and blowing on it gently.

Then she looked at me.

"What's the matter?" I asked idiotically, knowing full

well what the matter was.

"I know what'll happen when Annie gets back," she murmured, gazing up at the mountains.

"No, no, no," I lied transparently, realizing she was smarter than I was. "You don't have to worry—"

"No!" she bit her lip, putting her hand over mine as tears welled up. I could still score; I knew she loved me! I pressed the issue by moving closer and wrapping my arm around her; she pushed me away, self-absorbed, distant, in silent communion with something foreign to my bumbling, fumbling pubescent sensibility. Frightened by her tears, I was aware of being in the presence of a mature young woman who'd discovered self-respect right before my eyes.

Then shame washed over me—just for a moment, however. She stood up, brushing off her jeans. "Let's go back," she said.

I didn't want to go back. I discovered that I'd begun to feel about her the way she felt about me. At that moment, if someone offered me a paper consigning Annie to oblivion in my life, I would've signed it in a heartbeat. Then—quite suddenly—I felt cold all over. It wasn't that Mary Ann no longer cared for me—far worse. Rightly or wrongly, I was convinced that the thing Mary Ann loved in me had died an ignominious death.

And I had killed it.

> June 1
> Coming to take her
> A Chevy Nomad

The National Pastime

So baseball was considered in the mid-fifties, before NFL football climbed in the driver's seat.

I didn't know what "un-American" meant. If I did, I would've accused myself of that also.

The world's worst baseball player, nonetheless I asked Mrs. Sloane for permission to try out for the local Little League farm club for kids not good enough to make the big club. On the first day of practice, attended by some of my Covington classmates, I realized I'd made a terrible mistake. Was it only I who found a baseball too hard to catch, even in a glove?

"Don't throw it so fast," I told Ritchie Decker, a kid I was playing catch with. He laughed and threw harder (he became the team's ace pitcher.)

I struck out three times. Years later, when I heard the batter's lament "You can't hit what you can't see." I remembered that first day of practice which was also my last.

... My last time up to bat the pitcher walked two batters, and all eyes were on me. As I came to the plate I happened to see one of the coaches, a coarse thirty-something man named Chuck, toss a lit cigarette over his shoulder as he walked to the dugout. Following behind, his wife, a frumpy woman, the team "mom," picked up the cigarette from the dirt and continued puffing on it.

I swung futilely at the first two pitches; then the pitcher lost it again, throwing four straight balls. On first base—the bases were now loaded, no outs—I decided to grab one last chance to show my teammates "what you got."

Head down, ignoring the third base coach's signs, I took

off to steal second. The runner on the bag couldn't believe his eyes, but, panicked, he dashed for third. Hung out to dry, the kid on third headed for home. It was a rare triple play and the inning was over.

Then the screams began—from players, coaches, parents.

Riding my bike back to Twelve-acres in tears, I felt certain that not only was I congenitally unfit for baseball, I was unfit for life.

        In shadow
            Classmates in an old photo
                —Recognizing no one

        Red plastic radio—
            Triple to left center
                —Willie Mays

Moonrise

Leprous yellow moon—an old beggar required to carry a bell on a stick to warn others of his approach.

OK, forget the bell. But the leprosy effect seems real, thanks to the wrinkled Sea of Tranquility and the pockmarked lunar surface: clearly visible on this cloudless night.

Yep, I've sneaked out again, this time sans raincoat and warm clothes. I make my way down a narrow path through the bamboo forest to a tiny stream which, thanks to the rains, is full and running swiftly.

This is my favorite place at Twelve-acres. A tall stand of pussy willows half-fills the sky when I sit down; and the moon, tangled in the calligraphy of reeds and shadows, finally manages to rise and blot out the western stars.

Western! That word, not to mention its connotations, fascinates me. The mood doesn't last long (I have to get back before someone notices my empty bed), so I'm left to more mundane imaginings.

. . . Sitting there in the moonlight, where the path's infinity stops.

Lost in bamboo the stream and I divvy up nowhere

A MOMENT OF SLEEP

Prodigal moon, prodigal sun—
The sky—overcast for three straight days, with a spring shower here and there—mostly there, because my interest is always focused on the hills west of Twelve-acres, leap-frogging like children to the mountains.

What is it Melville calls clouds in *Moby Dick?* —*The gentle thoughts of the feminine air?* Or is that birds? As for the moon—

I like overcast skies best; blue skies, especially consecutive days of nothing but, bored me then and bore me now.

(Memo to the local TV weather guy: never mind your kit-bag of meteorological arcana—cut-off lows, sucker holes, pressure gradients—will we have interesting weather tomorrow? That's all that counts for me).

—And all that counted then, while clouds sneaked into my dreams as I, too, sneaked into the night: searching for Something which, it turns out, was searching for me—for all of us—with similar lack of success.

        Whispering
           The woman in the moon—
              So what brought me here?

Two Letters to My Mother

1.

Dear Mom,

Every time I flash back to the November night you died, other memories butt in, comprising a hall of funhouse mirrors: each one reflecting the warped image of a boy, an adolescent, and a young man: but always me.

In one (they don't occur in order), I'm riding a pony called Domino bareback, galloping through an orchard of cherry trees at Twelve-acres. In another, I'm walking down Emerson Street in Palo Alto, suitcase in hand, on my way to take the Greyhound bus up to Berkeley for my freshman year. In another, first day of school 1948, I'm climbing onto a school bus, looking over my shoulder at you looking at me. In another I'm schlepping that ugly gray and yellow suitcase up Hearst Street, heading for San Diego and my sophomore year in college.

In yet another... But you see the point. Like antechambers (to change the figure) these recollections have to be passed through (why does the passive voice seem so significant?) so that I may reach you. Or, to put it a very different way, so that I may leave you before you leave me.

> Day moon
> Rain on the gravestones
> —Things you wished for

2.

Dear Mom,

The other day on the phone Allan brought up the question I knew he'd ask one day: *Why did she send us away?*

Certainly the still waters of Allan's suffering run deeper than mine, because he went into exile more often: in Palo Alto, to the Turners across town for his kindergarten year; in Los Altos, to the a small foster home on Moody Road; three years later to Twelve-acres; back in Palo Alto, to the family of my high school chum and basketball teammate Ray Gale; in Berkeley, to Montana and the home of Agnes Corrigan, a distant family friend (that stay lasted three days); in tenth grade, to the Turners again, this time in Monterey, for one semester. . .

I accompanied him to just three of these places, but always, tied to me like a kite's tail (and, like a kite's tail, curiously steadying, rudder-like) is Allan's question: *Why?*

I told him the truth: I don't know, we'll never know, but in the back of my mind is the glimmer of a supposition: depression. I inherited your sense of humor; I know now that I must've also inherited your depressive tendencies. In 2012 we understand that depression is physiological, not merely situational; but back in the fifties, when the only mass drug for psychological disorders was something called Mil-town for anxiety (this was before Valium), if pursued by the black dog of depression you were pretty much on your own.

The natural egoism of children being what it is, I never wondered how Allan must've felt when he looked back at the receding shore of childhood and felt—how could he feel otherwise?—that his mother had abandoned him, not once, not twice. . . .His phone call was a key to at least one rusty lock of *Why*.

Someone wrote that there's an intimate connection between grief and sarcasm, sarcasm being a way of coping, but more than that a shield against the demons of regret and sorrow. Allan is by far the most sarcastic person I know, the second being myself.

. . . I felt I must say something. So I summoned up another memory—Allan doesn't remember it—of one day that you visited us at Twelve-acres.

As the car pulled in, seven-year-old Allan zoomed around a corner of the Big House, wearing a cowboy outfit, brandishing a toy gun, grinning from ear to ear.

Your face changed; your lips moved, struggling to say something. Then you blurted, "There's my baby!"

And you burst into tears.

    Slow seasons—
     Wonder Bread
      Liking Ike

Requiem I

Fourteen: that's how many suicides—friends, acquaintances, relatives of friends—I'm familiar with.

One jumped off the Bay Bridge; another off the Golden Gate; another off the top of a roof; still another threw herself from a skyscraper window in San Francisco. One hanged himself; nine shot themselves.

(The skyscraper jumper was my girlfriend Annie's mother. I had met her once during the first few weeks of my stay at Twelve-acres.)

One of the suicides, a fifteen-year-old boy in Berkeley, said to his mother as she held him, *I don't want to die.*

. . . Unbelievable—but there it is. Naturally I think of Dante's trees of the suicides in *The Divine Comedy*.

Winter trees, branches bereft of leaves—in a sunless corner of—where?

Dante's guess was as good as yours or mine.

Hell, Purgatory, or Paradise: in the shadows, tentative, furtive, rustling—the tragic wings of birds.

—White sky

Three in the morning

The moon is in shadow.

. . . This night at Twelve-acres I dream of giant insects climbing up the sides of skyscrapers—grasshoppers, praying mantises, ants, I forget which.

What god or goddess (so I wondered later on in life) created these bad boys?

. . . What strikes me is the lack of perspective in the dream. I'm not inside the building, so where am I? Floating in air; sitting on a sky-hook; gazing through heavy lenses from the roof of another skyscraper (the skyscraper Annie's mother leapt from?)

No, now I have it—the real question, I mean:
What was I?

      Eclipse
         How we know
             The darkness is darkness

Requiem II

    Who was it said, "The stone in my hand—it demands glory."?

    Yes, yes; but what good is that if, like the rest of us, the kid I was at Twelve-acres and the 70-year-old I am = David and Goliath rolled into one?

                    Summer dreams—
                          Lips I touch
                                  Never touching mine

The Lecture (1991)

In Lublin, Poland, where I'm serving as a Senior Fulbright Fellow, I give a series of lectures at the Catholic University, just down the street from my host school, the Marie Curie University. The audience is composed mostly of graduate students and faculty from both CU and MCU.

Before I begin my remarks, a woman approaches the podium, introduces herself as a Bulgarian visiting professor of American lit, and asks if her twelve-year-old daughter may attend. I say yes—adding that no doubt the poor kid will be bored to tears.

As I begin the lecture, I see this young girl—radiantly beautiful, with black hair tumbling around her shoulders—scribbling something on a piece of paper. She's a dead ringer for Annie, my long-ago girlfriend at Twelve-acres.

Good, I say to myself, figuring that she's keeping busy doodling or drawing.

Then, as I pace the stage directly in front of her, I look down and discover to my astonishment that she's taking notes (I can only imagine what an average American seventh-grader would be doing in her place).

On finishing my 90-minute talk, and after speaking with a few members of the audience individually, I pack up my briefcase and head downstairs to return to my apartment. As I reach the first floor and enter the quad, footsteps patter down behind me; turning, I see it's the twelve-year-old Bulgarian girl.

Snow has begun to fall. We stand there, looking at each other in silence for a few moments. Again I think of Annie.

Then she says,

"Why are you so rare?"

That's all. I'm dumbfounded; rarely at a loss for words, I've none. Finally I say something—don't remember what. A few more moments pass, the snow falls more heavily, the wind picks up, and I notice that she's shivering.

"Your mom will be wondering about you," I suggest; she nods soberly and holds out her hand. We shake hands; she scampers up the stairs—pausing once to wave at me—and disappears.

Age and circumstances notwithstanding, walking meditatively home in the falling snow I think I know how Dante must've felt when he first laid eyes on Beatrice.

      Gray ice—
         Slipping and giggling
            Two college girls

STRANGE INTERLUDE

—Loveless wraiths trekking the western sky?
Cumulonimbus clouds in search of—
For some reason, decades later (just last night, in fact) I recalled those talismanic clouds and how they sang harmony with my moods and memories—long after I left Twelve-acres.
Don't get me right. Not all my moods were gloomy—far from it.
Loveless waifs: ah, no.
I was never crazy about the word *waif;* in fact it was embarrassing to me. We kids at Twelve-acres were well-fed, well-housed, well-treated (at least until Mr. Bill arrived—more on him in a moment).
So: a boost from Baudelaire:
The clouds, the clouds, up there, the beautiful clouds—

    Famishing—
        Full moon
            Sky full of stars

Mr. Rice

An itinerant type, he bounced from job to job before being hired at Twelve-acres to be the maintenance guy.

Pay dirt, as he put it, was right around the corner.

Balding, heavy-set, he performed his duties adequately—but adequately wasn't enough for Mrs. Sloane. They butted heads a few times, until she ordered me to check up on him.

"She can keep her dress on," he said next to a dirt-pile, sweating and resting on a shovel.

"What did he say?" she demanded. "Tell me the truth."

I told her.

Next time I ran into him he said,

"I thought you were my friend."

I was consumed with guilt, feeling like a pawn on a chess board.

No matter. A week later he pulled up next to me as I walked with a dorm-mate. His back seat was crammed with luggage and clothes.

"I'll be back," he waggled a finger at me, grinning from ear to ear, "with a bulldog in the back seat and a blonde in the front. They can't keep Eddy Rice down!"

He was right.

> Gray sun
> —What
> Disappears

Opus zero

"You've changed."

I remember the words and where they were spoken—Twelve-acres, in the Big House—but I can't recall who spoke them, or why.

—Changed for better or worse? Probably the latter: in human life that's so often the case. But I don't know. Like all twelve-year-olds I experienced growing pains of the body and—*spirit* is the word that comes to mind, though it doesn't quite fit. . .

What does not change is the will to change.

At that moment in the Big House I drew a blank—or rather an inside straight in the imaginary poker game I played with myself (Mr. Rice had taught me poker), which beat the heck out of the pair of twos I started with. . .

You lose.

—But which *you?* By now you've gathered that my "self"—again the word seems awkward—wasn't palpable to me (I almost wrote palatable); only to others.

Certainly this is true of everyone to a degree; but in my case the need to look in the mirror and see No One ran pretty deep—like the swift-running creek in the bamboo forest which emptied into a river in a hurry to lose itself in the (changeless) Pacific.

    2014   One more winter   I re-introduce my selves

[Italicized line by Charles Olson]

Mnemosyne

Like previous generations of American popular culture, mine glommed onto hit songs on the radio (and fledgling TV programs like Dick Clark's *American Bandstand*), using them as memory-markers later on in life.

Maybe it's truer to say that we were used by them.

Anyway, and as I've suggested elsewhere, after a certain age all memory becomes masochistic: moments trapped in the amber of popular songs—*Rock Around the Clock; Black Slacks; Transfusion; Heartbreak Hotel; I Walk the Line*—tend to be the painful ones.

Forever attached to the morning after my close encounter with Sharon in the station wagon is Don Cherry's chart-buster *Band of Gold*—which, although we uttered a mutual *I love you,* Sharon was never destined to bestow on me!

As I was about to discover on a summer hike in the Santa Cruz Mountains (see below), melancholy is a two-edged sword, pain being a graffiti of the soul—a *Kilroy was here* assuring us that we were here, that we were definitely alive.

. . . *And* that, as Nietzsche says, if given the choice between feeling pain and nothing at all, human beings will choose pain every time.

Homer and Sophocles knew the secret: the meaning of the name Tiresias—the wise prophet who saw into the meaning of life—is *the weariness of rowing.*

Sixteen tons
What do you get?
Another day older
And deeper in debt

["Sixteen Tons": lyrics to the song by Tennessee Ernie Ford (1955)]

Nocturne

Sometimes at night, before drifting off to sleep, I pictured in my mind a magical eraser, blotting out as many possibilities from my future as I could imagine.

Not the future itself—just what physicists call world-lines which, I felt, couldn't happen precisely because I conceived of them.

Naturally most of these possibilities were dark; but not all . . .

If you hurt, my mother used to say, *think of something pleasant, like a birthday cake; that'll take your mind off the pain.*

Well, maybe. . .

Anyway—yes, I was superstitious: the same kid who, when I was six or seven, walked into a field west of my neighborhood with small squares of paper, brightly crayoned and folded. Then I snapped them high in the air with a rubber band—turning on my heel and walking away before they tumbled back to earth. If I didn't see them fall, I knew they'd made it to heaven.

(In my 70th year I still don't have to heart to tell him—)

Recently, the muse tried to rub out the above graffiti from my childhood memories by dropping this haiku in my lap:

> To heaven—
>   Above the song-bird's song
>   The song-bird's song

. . . At Twelve-acres, if I made sure the future remained

a tabula rasa, then—who knows? Maybe—

    Oops! I was about to write *Maybe the sky's the limit;* but no, that small boy in the field frowns and shakes his head—

    —Begging me to erase these words.

Two dreams of Annie

—In memoriam

1.

Death in summer...

Still, hardly anyone I know passed away in the warm months: always cold, stars hung like icicles from a dazzling moon.

... Wandering through a meadow crisscrossed with shadows and sunlight; clouds, benignly indifferent, march from horizon to horizon: sheep following the leader in solemn foolery.

—As I sit alone in the tall grass she approaches, tossing a lock of hair from her eyes. Her hair is so dark it's almost blue, like the rich earth of Minnesota where she was born before moving to California and Twelve-acres.

The disease ticking inside her is unknown to both of us.

She sits down next to me and takes my hand while a meadowlark, startled by our presence, sings seven bright notes of warning.

It's the same song I heard when very young, before foster homes came into my life: dozing on a summer morning, window open, all the world's kindness, certitude, comfort, joy, and yes faith, in the breeze that filled my curtains.

    Sound of a waterfall
      —On her shoulder
          A glass-wing butterfly

2.

Wan yellow...

The sun rises behind my eyelids, and the country I'm wandering through this night begins to brighten: its lone valley, spotted with live-oaks, yawning and stretching like a young leopard.

What is she doing right now? Oh, but I know: turning in bed, eyes open, gazing at the east window brimming with oranges, yellows, and pale pinks: her own dreams fleeing like ghosts into the comfort of the room's dark corners, singing, *"Good-bye—don't forsake us!"*

And I know the point that must be reached is the point of no return.

> Cries and whispers
>   What we say
>   What we hear

Twelve-acres
II

CRIMES AND MISDEMEANORS

Summers Twelve-acres morphed into a church camp: children from all over California attended, and we full-time foster kids moved from the dorms down to the swimming pool area, into big tents pitched on wooden platforms.

The camp director was a humorless martinet named Bill from up in Berkeley. First thing he did was to issue an order that campers must address adults, counselors and staff alike, with Mr. or Miss tacked on to their first name.

I declared war on him after he went after Allan, my younger brother, with a belt. I forget most of what I did or didn't do, but poolside one hot afternoon I pushed Miss Margaret, the assistant director, into the water. A kindly soul and a good sport, she didn't seem to mind, surfacing and giggling as other kids looked on in amazement.

Then Mr. Bill showed up. I don't remember what my punishment was—not much, probably: exile to a dark room in the recreation hall. For some reason he spared me the belt.

—Fast-forward six years to the spring of 1962, when I was a freshman at Cal, a member of the "Org"—Christian Science Organization for students. (But I was on the clock: a few weeks later I got the heave-ho after being caught in the chaperon's apartment with a visiting high school senior from Mill Valley named Donna).

One Sunday after church they threw a party with Kool-aide and cookies in the lobby. Sure enough, there was Mr. Bill, a tad grayer around the temples, chatting with the chaperon and a few students. At his elbow: a beautiful young brunette wife, whom I'd never seen before.

I walked up to him and asked if he remembered me.

Mr. Bill looked me up and down coldly, as if I'd sprayed shit-mist about the lobby.

Then, with the same false heartiness he once displayed with parents of campers:

"—Twelve-acres!"

He extended his hand; I refused to shake it.

Looking on, the wife smiled a little—a knowing smile?

I turned away and left, heading back to my Parker Street apartment in the spring sunshine.

Here's the strange part. Walking under the cherry trees south on Bowditch, I was puzzled that my anger had incubated all these years—until I realized the real issue had little to do with Twelve-acres.

No—I was angry because Mr. Bill had such a gorgeous young wife: to my callow eighteen-year-old sensibility, definitely a rift in the cosmic scheme of things.

> Fading birdsong
> What we might've been

Lost

We marched along, a cohort of tired church-campers in the Santa Cruz Mountains.

One of the counselors at Twelve-acres, a pretty girl whose name I've long forgotten, began to sing the song *Cool, Clear, Water,* waving one arm like an orchestra conductor.

Someone hushed her.

Although I was thirsty I didn't mind her singing. It seemed like something I could crawl into, under a fantasy sky of lyric starlight and thunder over nearby Mt. Hamilton.

That we'd lost our bearings didn't seem to matter.

The wind picked up, a violent tango of live-oak leaves dancing around us, accompanied by a fine brown talc of dust. Just as suddenly the wind died down, and we trudged on.

. . . Ahead, chatting with a counselor was a "girlfriend," Beverley, a tall, tanned, frizzy-haired sixth-grader from San Diego. I was in puppy love (again).

(Btw, never gainsay puppy love. Its disappointments—its bark and bite—hurt every bit as much as adult love.)

I'd grown up with these mountains—gazed at them from my back yard in Palo Alto, thirty-plus miles away. In the late afternoon their blues and purples filled me with melancholy—not wholly unpleasant.

In fact, over time it, the melancholy, became a form of sustenance, something I grew to depend on, almost like a drug.

I know now that what I was feeling was the stirrings of PTSD, which kicked in after my father's death in 1950.

Of course this seemed odd until, years later, I read an

account by a well-known victim of autism.

In spite of her affliction she earned a PhD in animal sciences and went on to become a world-renowned expert on and advocate for humane treatment of cattle. Lecturing on autism in a flat, emotionless tone, she acknowledged the condition's terrible limitations before adding that she wouldn't change a thing.

Autism, she claimed, wasn't something she had; it was something she was.

I feel the same way about PTSD—did so age twelve, although I couldn't articulate it.

But now that I was in the blue and purple mountains I'd always seen *from a distance,* I was bereft of the feelings of melancholy tangled up with pleasurable mysteries of their cold colors and fortuitous shadows: orchestrated by No One.

I felt cheated.

> Full moon
> Cry
> Of a raven

Song for Edmond

    Shadowing
        Each other's shadows—
      Live-oaks

Oh, yes: we—along with how many others before and after?—were responsible.

His name was Edmund Otis Pew: strikes one, two, and three on the playground and in the classroom.

—Overweight, wimpy, unhappy, all we fellow Twelve-acres campers could think of was how to make things worse for him.

(What irked us in particular was an irritating habit of Edmund's. He would fold his oversized polka-dot kerchief over and over until it almost disappeared. Only then could he go to sleep.)

(Kids are super-insensitive to their sensitive brethren, and we would make rabbit ears to Edmund with our fingers to signify that he was too quick—too eager?—to hear things we shamelessly whispered about him.)

In the beginning we tossed pebbles in his glass of Kool-Aid—"bug juice"—at lunchtime. Then we spread a rumor around camp that a breed of spiders liked to lay their poisonous eggs in sleeping bags, where it was nice and warm. The counselors—campers themselves once upon a time—laughed the rumor off, putting it in the same category as snipe hunts.

. . . Lights out in two minutes: Edmund (he was in the bunk below mine) slipped on a pair of bright green pajamas and crawled into his bag, only to discover the salmon eggs we'd planted there.

To this day I've never heard a shriek as loud. One cohort four rows of tents down said it woke him up from a sound sleep.

Still in pajamas, barefoot and shrieking, Edmund flew out of the tent and disappeared into the night.

> Turning the other cheek
> To her dark side—
> Summer moon

No one found him, and so he stayed somewhere until dawn, when two counselors discovered Edmund under a live-oak tree, curled up in the fetal position.

His mother showed up late in the afternoon (I didn't know about a stepfather until later), and took him back to Palo Alto. I never saw Edmund again.

Fast forward five years to when I'm in high school.

I'm flipping through the *Palo Alto Times* when I come across the news item.

The day before, Edmund Pew (who, it turns out, lived only eight blocks from me on Waverly Street) had patiently spent two hours on the front porch, waiting for his stepfather to come home from work.

When the stepfather finally showed up Edmund whipped out the shotgun he'd hidden behind him.

—And brought it to his shoulder. —And aimed it. —And fired both barrels, sending his stepfather's cranium into a pile of autumn leaves across the street.

Childlike in so many ways, Edmund was now old enough to be tried as an adult. His lawyer's insanity plea went nowhere.

Shortly afterward, the mother left town.

—And so, fifty-plus years later, sitting on Swan Lake's rocky beach, all I can do for Edmund is toss pebble after pebble—

Before the icy water folds over and the pebbles disappear.

                Violet star
                      A guard on the tower
                              Shoots at a rabbit

Outward bound

The number one song that summer was *The Wayward Wind*.

On field trips, including the one to the Santa Cruz Mountains, we sang it on the bus. My vocal cords had yet to change and I had a fair to middling voice.

The song haunted my dreams and waking hours—

In a lonely shack by a railroad track
He spent his younger days;
And I guess the sound of the outward bound
Made him a slave to his wandering ways—

—That was the season of another New York Yankees pennant (Mickey Mantle would win the Triple Crown). In the cocoon of summer camp, though, I was unaware of everything else in the outside world—history, as usual, was being made in the Middle East, but the Gaza Strip might as well have been on the dark side of the moon as far as I was concerned.

I'd become introspective that year, asking the same ontological questions all adolescents wrestle with—what is it that makes me different from the others? A born worrywart, I spent hours in a perpetual frown, contemplating my future beyond Twelve-acres. Would there be more foster homes? Why were my brother and I sent here in the first place? Etc.

Years later, at the Org in Berkeley, I ran into Miss Helen, a counselor at Twelve-acres that summer; she was a senior English major, living in sorority row up on Piedmont Street.

She promised to bring her scrapbook to the next Wednesday night "testimony meeting" and, afterward, we sat in the lobby and flipped through it.

. . . There we all were, bathed in summer sunlight shining on the nothing new of adolescence—shining, that is, on kids who felt they were the first ones to discover sex. As usual a scowl darkened my tanned face.

Suddenly Helen turned to me.

"You were *so nice*," her face lit up in a smile.

I was? This was news to me; I didn't remember being "nice" at all. Certainly Edmund Pew wouldn't have thought so.

. . . Later, back in my apartment, and not for the first or last time, in the mirror I was re-introduced to the stranger disguised with my face.

       Echo of a dream
          Abyss
              Of a dream

Journey to a Small Planet

By the time summer rolled around I'd had plenty of time to discover the extensive library located on the third floor of the Big House.

I spent hours there during the winter and spring, and even now, during free time at camp, I dashed back up to the nearly deserted House, climbed the stairs, and borrowed a book or two to take to my tent.

Do kids read the Tom Swift series anymore? The last volumes appeared in 1981, so I suppose there's a few out there who can be temporarily weaned off computers, smart phones, and video games.

Anyway, I'd stumbled on the Victor Appleton volumes (V.A. was a pseudonym) earlier that year. Most of the books were old, so I suspected the library had been left behind by previous owners.

Prowling the stacks—it was actually set up like a real library—I was in heaven. Still, to call my voracious appetite for books escapism would've been too easy. In some ways the opposite was true. The sci-fi worlds of Tom Swift and of Dorothy, Toto, and Oz—which I'd fallen for at an earlier age—were so real to me that at times the day-world of Twelve-acres, even of Covington Junior High, seemed dream-like.

If a few things were still unpleasant (it was January when a housemother first showed me the library), nonetheless I'd more or less settled in.

Books like the early Robert A. Heinlein series—*Farmer in the Sky, The Green Hills of Earth,* and *Red Planet*—also appealed to me: my dreams began to feature aliens, starships, and distant planets with two suns in the sky.

A handful of these dreams persisted into adulthood, "updated" with persons, places, and things which had swum into my ken during the intervening years.

Here's my most recent dream; the original version goes back sixty years:

I've landed on a world, third from the two suns of a system 600 light-years away: like our earth a blue-green orb bathed in oxygen and nitrogen.

Two twilights: one tequila-colored, the other burnt orange, and the purple shadows of rocks elongating, then shrinking, elongating and shrinking yet again, all within two hours' time.

And a necklace of moons—turquoise, green, silver-gray, dark yellow—and sentient, intelligent floating flowers, based not on chlorophyll but compassion!

. . . Awakening to a terrestrial desert morning of creosote fragrance, tears of raindrops suspended from saguaro spines, the old pleasant feeling of melancholy hangs on from last night's dream.

        Entangled
           In live-oak branches
                The dawn star

Epilogue

I still don't know what moved me to do it.

Fall 1956: Upon returning home to Palo Alto after the year at Twelve-acres, I felt an urge—was it a need?—to re-visit the group home. Maybe it was because my most recent experience had been summer camp which, in spite of Mr. Bill, turned out to be fun.

Or maybe because, like all thirteen-year-olds (my birthday is August 29), I wasn't the same kid who came to Twelve-acres the previous fall.

I also liked the challenge of riding my bicycle from Palo Alto to Los Altos: pretty far on two wheels but I knew it could be done. (More than once at Twelve-acres it occurred to me to hop on my bike and head to 3216 Emerson St. in Palo Alto, although I knew Mom would've sent me back.)

Early one Saturday morning I was off, taking a route I've forgotten except that it skirted the Stanford hills, wending southwest to Los Altos. I arrived just before noon. Naturally the first person I encountered was Mrs. Sloane—I'd hoped to avoid her, not because she was the ogre Mr. Bill was, but she was such a stickler for rules I worried that she would turn me around.

I wasn't part of Twelve-acres any more—and yet . . .

Mrs. Sloane wasn't particularly welcoming; neither did she send me away—inviting me, in fact, to join the kids for lunch. Summer campers were long gone, with them Beverley; so were Annie, Sharon, and Mary Ann; but I knew most of the others—they were curious as to why I was there.

So was I.

After lunch we trooped down to the swimming pool—I'd

brought my swim suit—and jumped in. I wanted to repeat my "triumphs" of summer, when I was the best diver and one of the best swimmers. It didn't work. The water seemed to be resisting me—seemed heavier, somehow, clinging to my legs and arms, as if I were trying to swim through green Jell-O.

What's happening to me?

This was the same medium that, only a few short months ago, had buoyed me up—I remember feeling cradled as I won swimming races—while the others and Miss Margaret looked on. Not now.

(I thought of Sharon resisting me—and the eternal mornings after . . .)

Why had Twelve-acres (the pool seemed metonymic) turned on me—as I had once turned on it? Having enrolled in what seemed my umpteenth school back in Palo Alto, I was now a stranger in two lands which, far from being strange, were quite familiar.

After I got dressed and climbed on my bike for the long ride home, Mrs. Sloane came up to me. I could see she was choosing her words carefully.

"It was good to see you, Steve," she said without enthusiasm. "But I have to tell you . . ." Pause. Then, kindly: "This should be your only visit."

—Fast-forward thirty years.

Allan and I pay a visit to the Turners in Palo Alto, with whom Allan had spent time as a boy. Then we decide to tool over to Twelve-acres . . .

It's gone, torn down—even the Big House and most of the live-oak trees have vanished. In their place: a tony upscale housing development called Twelve-acres.

Forgotten sunsets—
      Same song
            Different meadowlark

Postscript

Not to make invidious comparisons between Class A and Class C—but I'm always struck by similarities between Herman Melville's childhood and mine.

We both lost our fathers early; we were both voracious readers when very young; we both had poor eyesight; we both had extensive periods of rootlessness; etc.

This is why, I suppose, I flashed on the following paragraph from one of Melville's little-read novels.

I feel certain he was thinking of his own boyhood:

Talk not of the bitterness of middle-age and after life; a boy can feel all that, and much more, when upon his young soul the mildew has fallen; and the fruit, which with others is only blasted after ripeness, with him is nipped in the first blossom and bud. And never again can such blights be made good; they strike in too deep, and leave such a scar that the air of Paradise might not erase it. And it is a hard and cruel thing thus in early youth to taste beforehand the pangs which should be reserved for the stout time of manhood, when the gristle has become bone, and we stand up and fight out our lives, as a thing tried before and foreseen; for then we are veterans used to sieges and battles, and not green recruits, recoiling at the first shock of the encounter.

Book II

Steven/Peter

"Oh, Steven, there always seems to be two of you."
—V.K., 1965

[N.B.: Words of the vertical poems attached to some of the prose passages below alternate between Steven and Peter. The reader is invited to decide which of the two vertical poems in each "set" belongs to whom.]

OVERTURE

Acutely aware of being bounded in a nutshell of earthly distances; weary of being a prisoner of gravity and the capriciousness of grace—
—Weary of weariness itself, my doppelganger stumbles out of bed.
And checks out the sky from horizon to horizon—a Japanese bowl lacquered with calligraphies of winter branches and moonlight.
Except—guess what? We're not in Japan! We're right here: smack dab in the Sonora Desert, on the 17th of February 2014. I watch my doppelganger watch the heavens. Who is he anyway?
(I'd better give him a name—*Peter*).
Is he the one who whispers the lies I want to hear?
Or vice versa—truths I don't want to hear? Is he the one with tears in his eyes during Carmen's death scene in the ballet we saw yesterday at the Temple of Music and Art?
—Or is Peter a she? Maybe these whispers come from the yin and yang within all of us. . .

Bright
—Hour
Reds
Of
Starving
The
In
Wolf
A

Feasting
Dark
On
Sky
Darkness

1.

Peter's the guy who shrugs off PTSD and does things I can't, or won't.

I wonder if doppelgangers are "multiple"—if the double is made up of more than one entity. So, for example, the kindness Peter showed to the distraught Mrs. Davidson at Twelve-acres also came from my (our) father, who was known for his compassion (toward Japanese-Americans during the War, among many others).

What about Peter's feelings for a lost girl back in the day, who wouldn't listen to reason but inexplicably wrote many years later: *You're part of my heart?* Or was she the ghost (remember the yin and yang!) of a lost boy from my mother's past, a naval aviator killed in a plane crash? Peter can't say, and neither can I.

        Bridge
        Cold
        Too
        Pale
        Narrow
        Purple
        For
        Shadows
        Two

2.

Peter wanted to play piano.

—Even as I wanted to play professional basketball (although it was Peter who, after being cut from the UC freshman basketball team, walked back to the Parker Street apartment with tears in his eyes).

It's Peter who wanted to learn Sanskrit; Japanese; Klingon—

. . . So I wonder if that's what joins doppelgangers at the hip—regret upon regret, like mountains upon mountains receding in the distance—

—Until infinity comes to a stop.

River
Always
Rising
The
River
Darkness
Falling

3.

So what will I—what will Peter—miss the most?

I've written elsewhere that in the afterlife, if one exists, for sure I'll miss autumn leaves—brilliant flags in the ranks of death.

For his part, Pete will miss the agony and the ecstasy—yes, the agony too—of falling in love.

In this I'm one up on him. Why? There're only two things in life no one else can do for you: dying and falling in love. Dying is easier.

. . . But maybe it's death itself we will both miss the most—the exhilarating risk of death which gets us off our duffs and into the world: where the beauty of chaotic phenomena—ocean waves, blossom-storms, the shifting colors of dawn—reprograms the lateral geniculate nucleus in the thalamus.

Aerobics, so to say, for the brain cells: a passel of endorphins thrown in for good measure.

Biologically speaking, this is why we love ocean-gazing, cloud-watching, birds in flight, etc.

So I check out hawks circling the hill shadowing our ravine: death-wishes bumping the glass ceiling of heaven.

Here I sit, a prisoner of the green earth, sipping my third cup of coffee.

Green, green—it's green they say, on the far side of the hill—
I think of Peter's gentleness and commit the sin of envy!

Clinging
***Circles*—**
To

Yet
One
The
Wild
Same
Rose:
Circle—
Crane
Red-tailed
Mountain
Hawks

[*Green, green.* . . Song lyrics by the New Christy Minstrels]

4.

It's the constancy of the speed of light (186,000 miles/second) that we love. Light-speed itself would drive Peter and me insane.

Warp Factor Zero, for God's sake, Scottie.

(We think of time as the essence of Normalcy. But if clocks could think they too would go bonkers.)

All this intrigues me. There are other constants in the universe: Planck's and the Gravitational. They're "inhuman," existing separate from our prayers, loves, words, not to say the vanity of human wishes.

As for doppelgangers—

Oops! Let's not forget the Big Bang itself (a she or a he?), soon to be followed in cosmic time by the Big Whimper.

Listen, writes E.E. Cummings, *there's a hell of a good universe next door. Let's go.*

. . . Reminding Peter and me of the film *Annie Hall* in which, as a child, the Woody Allen character refuses to do his homework, arguing that if the expanding universe will break up billions of years from now, why bother? (Peter got a huge kick out of that one).

Well, here I am, aforementioned prisoner of the green earth and of my own constants: three cups of coffee, two hours squabbling with the computer until eleven a.m. when it's down to the bar for FOX News and a glass of Brownstone Chard. But first I—I mean Peter—will kick things off with a Tanqueray and tonic.

. . . Suddenly a cloud blots out the last pinks and yellows of dawn; as I finish my coffee, another constant—or rather a realization—taps me on the shoulder:

The Big Bang and Big Whimper, too, are doppelgangers.
The music of the spheres in silent harmony—

> Why
> **Silent**
> Are
> **Choir**
> We
> **Of**
> Here
> **Headstones**

5.

A tad more skeptical than I, Peter asks:

"But, Steven, what is the Big Bang but a creation myth, nothing more nothing less?"

Mm . . . The universe isn't infinite (is it?). Elsewhere, and, even as Keats drank death to Newton for explaining the rainbow, I wrote: *Death (or at least a bad cold) to Einstein for explaining curved space, thus obliterating distance!*

—*To hold infinity in the palm of your hand*—

Peter completes Blake's thought, sort of:

—*And the woman in the moon in a glass of Chardonnay.*

    Waiting
    The
    For
    Pain
    The
    Of
    Lighthouse
    Feeling
    Flash
    No
    Empty
    Pain
    Ocean

6.

Not the music of the spheres but . . .

Peter—he's more musical than I—played the triangle in our second grade classroom "orchestra."

A zillion years later the memory of that—along with tinnitus—still titillates my own ear.

As Lascaux cave-bison would be the first to tell you, suffering is an art form, re-shaping the world in a new way.

Btw, never believe any of that about redemptive suffering. Suffering is redemptive only for those who never suffer.

But I regress.

Don't get me right: I'm not talking about how suffering leads to art, which of course it does. No: I'm talking about *in the beginning*—

In the beginning there was light. Why? So we could know that dark is dark, for God's sake.

Peter quotes Don Paterson:

We turn from the light to see.

Deep
Morning
In
Shadows
The
Take
Woods
Me
Fireflies
For
In

A
Love
Walk

7.

When the gods came up with tenderness, certainly they had women in mind—but it's not that simple.

Steven: Why do women crave—adore—tenderness in men?
Peter: Because men hold up their own tenderness to them as in a mirror.

If the shoe were on the other foot, this would be blatant egotism—egotism and egoism. Narcissus was a boy not a girl.

—Ah, but in *women* . . .

Let's put it this way. Women respond to male tenderness in the same way that the Renaissance God appeared to respond to the entire Creation He made.

Peter quotes Thomas More:

He made the plants to show Him simplicity. He made the animals to show him innocence. But He made man so that, in the tangle of his mind, he might learn to create—

Peter trails off, so this time I have the last word:

The rest is silence.

Desert
Dawn—
Moonlight
Half-asleep
Three a.m.
I
I
Forget
Hear

To Munch's ***Think*** *The* ***About*** *Scream* ***Death***

8.

The Egyptians believed that the sun was re-born each morning, having spent the night in the breast of the goddess who morphed into Aphrodite.

Naturally this brings a smile to Peter's face.

(I myself wear a perpetual frown—a never-ending source of embarrassment to me. The other day at the bar someone asked, half-alarmed: "Are you OK, Steve?")

Where were we? Oh, yes—

. . . We moderns knock on wood to solicit the assistance of Dryads. And we pluck flower-petals in order to "read" the heart of another: *She loves me not, she loves me not—*

For the Egyptians there was also "Our Lady of the Sycamore," who concealed herself in the foliage of sycamores on the edge of the desert. In her custody was a long ladder which the deserving could ascend to heaven.

For me—for my adult self—I've always thought of dawn (Eos) as a courtesan: all rouged up.

Now it's Peter's turn to frown!

—The stars wink out one by one and I feel jealous.

I mean, what are those bad boys up to, as the sun—Ra, Helios, Tenerife, Ravi, Sol, Hors— ticks down the sky?

Gentlemen and ladies, we have met the courtesan and she is us.

Speak for yourself, says Peter.

        Our
        Promiscuous
        Lady
        Colors

Of
Of
The
Twilight
Cantina

9.

Naturally her name reminds me of Malcolm Lowry's haunting refrain *Dolor, Dolente* (in the novel *Under the Volcano*).

At lunchtime Dolores and I stop by a Greek place for sandwiches and walk up to Union Square.

The weather—this is summer, '66—is perfect most days. Sitting on the grass, eating the Greek sandwiches and fending off greedy pigeons, we talk about everything under the San Francisco sun, including my Giants—destined to lose yet another pennant race—and the recent mass killings in Texas and Chicago: first in a series. . .

Thin—a little too thin for my jaded palate—but very pretty, Dolores has a crush on me. Or is it Peter? Once, impulsively, she reaches out and touches my hair.

"It sparkles in the sunlight," she murmurs shyly, turning to watch a mime performing on the impromptu Union Square stage.

Spotting Dolores touch my hair he smiles, nods, and touches his heart.

Like the mime, Peter says nothing.

Around that time I fall for a beautiful model who works at Macy's, four blocks from where Dolores and I sit. Tall, leggy, blonde, she holds my hand as we walk to work from the bus station (Dolores lives in the City, the blonde and I across the Bay).

When I ask this other girl out, she drops a bomb: She's Mormon and can't date outside her religion. Later she writes me, saying the same thing in more detail.

So there we are, Dolores and I: balanced by Peter's lack

of passion for her and the model's lack of passion for me.

    The summer of our discontent, made inglorious winter by—

        The scales of desire!

> Thou
> ***Letter***
> Shalt
> ***Explaining***
> Not
> ***Why***
> Be
> ***We***
> Melted
> ***Could***
> By
> ***Never—***
> Her
> ***Postage***
> Frozen
> ***Due***
> Smile

10.

Let's revisit the two meanings of *dear:* well-loved and costly.

Naturally Peter prefers the former.

Cantilever of souls! One single word—

No matter. Number, Pythagoras believed, allows us to gate-crash the mind of God.

I see him standing on the shore of Samos: fascinated as the wall of blue sky and the line of ocean intersect each other—at a right angle!

As for death's dear and delicate arithmetic—

2 (Peter and myself) + X (so many inamoratas) = O.

Undo the math, dear friend.

Thin
Leaf-shapes
Thinner
Of
Thinnest
Empty
Winter
Sky
Light

11.

It just occurred to me—yes, I'm a slow thinker—that I write better in the dark, not to say *about* the dark.

No need to wax melodramatic about this—it is what it is. *Fewer distractions* Peter interjects—again showing a practical streak. *That's why.*

True, but dawn and daylight bring with them their own poems: the good, the bad, and the ugly.

To me darkness is alive in a way that light—the world of light—is not. Let me reprise a poem Peter and I co-wrote after a night of intermittent jottings-down in my bed-stand notebook:

When I slide my bedroom window open at four a.m., I hear the sound of breathing.

—Where?

—The ridge, holding the lavenders and blues of day hostage?

—The ravine, expressway for white-tailed deer (and, I'm told, mountain lions, though I've never seen one)?

Or—

Is the darkness itself breathing, reassuring us that Gaia will make it through another night sans religion, booze, or a lover?

I go back to bed. At five-thirty Eos—darling girl!—pays a hefty ransom, releasing the colors back to earth and sky.

Welcome!

(Needless to say, the last three lines are Peter's.)

Dreaming
Shaping
I'm
Loneliness—

Dreaming
Twilight
I'm
Bell

12.

Yep, it happens—thunder in the midst of a snowstorm.

Who knew? You say—and yet, thanks to the gods (bored to tears on Olympus) there are stranger weathers—frogs scooped up by a tornado and deposited on the heads of Ohio townspeople thirty miles away; the year without a summer in New England (1816); etc.

The TV blinks and my baseball game disappears. Bored with sports, Peter could care less.

Remember—Zeus wasn't the head honcho on Olympus. That role was reserved for Destiny, who made the rules governing salvation.

Peter isn't particularly impressed with my definition of salvation:

A game postponed indefinitely due to whether . . .

13.

Like you, I'm sick to death of marketing calls, especially at dinnertime.

Last night the phone rings during dessert.

"*. . . How are you today? I have important information—*"

"How am I today?" I cut him off with a lie. "I'll tell you how I am today. This afternoon I was diagnosed with stage four cancer of the bile duct."

—Long, very long, silence.

(Blushing with embarrassment, Peter glares at me: "Steven—for heaven's sake!").

"*. . . I'm sorry to hear that, sir. May I speak to your wife? I have important—*"

14.

DNA—

Kids, Do Not Attempt this at home—

Attempt what? —Russian roulette? —Mexican food roulette (family legend had it that my maternal great grandfather—actually he was Portuguese—ate his way into the grave)?

I'm not sure what genetic legacies in me trump these domestic games of roulette—my DNA hiding in the tall weeds, ready to pounce like a tiger.

Peter: "Excuse me, buddy—our DNA!"

Hold the phone! Doctors now say that 72 = the new 30.

Peter: "What a relief!"

Or is it? Suppose we were granted immortality?

Two schools of thought kick in:

—We'd morph into the listless, miserable creatures Swift envisions in *Gulliver's Travels,* whose lives have no purpose—the purpose(s) limned by mortality. *Save us, with birthdays,* a poet writes—who died young.

—We'd adapt to the prospect, discovering new talents, new resiliencies—perhaps new evolutionary protocols. At some point instrumentality, even the mortal coil of flesh, might be selected out of human existence: indeed, the line between matter and spirit might gradually disappear . . . In other words, no rules, no game.

I don't know. Even now, most loves don't last "forever," as the Valentine cards say.

And rainbows get boring, so that, wine-glass empty Peter and I turn away and head indoors . . .

Cold
Blowing
Comforter
Out
Of
The
Spring
Candles
Snow

15.

Now—right now—*No two snowflakes alike* seems to Peter a tyranny. Not that he'd want them all the same . . .

As for me, I—the mystery of "I"—hover like a devil's moth between *No two alike* and *All the same*.

Why? Why this particular difference between us?

Peter: "I don't want to go there!"

. . . A friend from up north says Swan Lake is finally frozen over. Now red foxes, eagles and even a moose or two will appear: foxes and eagles drawn by the carcass of a deer dragged to the center of the lake by my neighbor Don, astride his small John Deere tractor.

Who says there's no free lunch?

As for the moose—years ago Don saw one fall through the ice, struggle mightily, and climb back to safety.

I ask my friend what else is going on.

It's snowing hard, he says. *Man, it's like being in a waterfall—coming down so fast you can't see the flakes.*

No flakes—are you sure?

Would I lie to you?

> In
> **Here**
> The
> ***Lie***
> Mirror—
> ***Steven***
> A
> ***And***
> Stranger

***Peter*—**
Disguised
Solved
With
By
My
The
Face
Mystery

16.

The difference between childhood and adulthood: in childhood words don't get in the way of experience.

(Peter reminds me of the anecdote about Oliver Wendell Holmes, who didn't talk until he was five. Finally, over dinner one night, he said: "The soup's cold."

His astonished parents asked, "Why didn't you say anything before?"

"Nothing was wrong before.")

—Anyway, things just happen—to be put in mind storage for future retrieval. In adulthood, no matter how "transparent," the words do get in the way; and the poor writer, slave to his only medium, must do his best.

"Amen to that," Peter adds.

17.

For all these egoistical romps, but to be fair to Peter, I should repeat that I've always been in love with the NOT ME—the Siren-song of otherness as sung to us by Ma Nature.

"Siren-song" is a stretch, because otherness is neutral—it too a universal constant of sorts. Forgiving and unforgiving, its favorite incognito is the ocean, mirroring the souls of sailors drowned and rescued, the drowned crying for their mums, even as they return to the Womb of their spawning.

And because, God damn it, cliché or no we persist in being strangers to ourselves (no offense, Pete).

18.

Just last night, a few short hours ago, I had a terrible dream.

Peter and I are back in Palo Alto in the fifties, alone in the house on Emerson Street. All the furniture is there, including the green plastic couch with stuffing coming out of the seams.

It's Peter who seems more upset—embarrassed—by this. He finds a red Tot stapler and tries—unsuccessfully—to hide the rips and tears.

(In the dream a flashback: a lady from the Aid to Needy Children agency rings the doorbell and my mother lets her in. She's very nice but I resent her—so much so that I embarrass Peter and my mom by being rude—as if simple rudeness could or would alter my destiny!)

. . . Anyway, through the west window—next to the warped door which I perpetually struggled with, so that I was always afraid the window would shatter—I see the antediluvian back yard fence, bowing reverentially toward a sun low in the sky.

I wander from room to room. The front yard, which I can see from my old bedroom window, still features what's left of a pine tree my mother and I planted in 1957. Clouds mount in the east, putting me in mind of polar bears rearing up on their haunches.

Then a car pulls into the driveway, followed by a moving van; a 1950s'-style family, young parents and the obligatory two kids, flock to the door, chattering and laughing. The movers begin to unload furniture.

They can't see me; no matter, since now I'm on my knees

scooping up ashes in the fireplace with a dustpan, depositing them in a cardboard box, coughing and sneezing. Behind me, the kids dash from room to room in their new home, still laughing.

I despise this family, but just as I'm about to say something to the parents, they've vanished, to be replaced by another family pulling up outside; then another, then another.

Peter begins to weep.

Like the eastward clouds, my rage mounts; but before I can do violence to this farrago of innocent strangers, I wake up, sweating.

    Dying
    Roots
    Jack-
    Above
    Pine
    Ground

19.

Last night, singing into a mirror: the Italian tenor on TV's *Classic Arts Showcase*.

As the camera zeroed in on his reflection, I was reminded of an aphorist's "What I have given you is not what you receive."

(This has become a mantra between Peter and me).

So what *do* Peter's and my reflections receive—rather, what do they give back to us? Not "ourselves" obviously; but—

When I look in the mirror I see Peter; when Peter looks he sees me.

Two passages:

—*As he passed in the way of the cheval-glass, he caught sight of himself in full length, his broad, well-filled shirt-front, the face whose expression always puzzled him when he saw it in a mirror...*

—*On his way back to the living room he passed a mirror in the dining room and looked at it. His face looked strange. He smiled at the face in the mirror and it grinned back at him. He winked at it and went on. It was not his face but it didn't make any difference.*

You see the point.

Or do you—the "point," too, being a mirror!

Let's give the final solo in this warped chorus to Jean Cocteau—

Mirrors always reflect more than we want them to.

Peter: *More, of course, being less...*

[The two passages: the first by James Joyce from *The Dead*, the second by Ernest Hemingway from *The Three-Day Blow*]

20.

Peter: Folks, I'm addicted to nonsense in no way, shape or form. It's Steven who "swatted up" as the Brits say a literature course called the Anatomy of Nonsense, and taught it at the University of Arizona eons ago. —*Alice in Wonderland, Catch-22, A Midsummer Night's Dream,* etc.

Steven: *Tell me the truth,* I implored her—and got just what I deserved . . .

Two
Truths
Bear
Merely
Witness
Exchange
To
One
The
Set
Truth:
Of
One
Shackles
Speaks
For
It,
Another;
One
Nonsense
Turns

Sets
A
You
Deaf
Free—
Ear
Truly!

21.

Love thyself as thy neighbor—
—Or as thy doppelganger?
—Recipe for salvation or damnation? The issue, as Peter would say, is finely balanced.

For example, at the bar, on a dark afternoon when I'm in a good mood:

How are you? I murmur to an imperfect stranger—someone I barely know. Saying these words I hear the phoniness in my voice, and literally shudder. Is this me? Is this the best I'll come up with on the mean streets of Purgatory?

She replies sincerely and with a smile: *How are you?*
Not too well, my introspective self is tempted to say.
—Peter smiles ironically: *But that, of course, would be sincere—*

Sometimes I wish he would keep his big mouth shut.

22.

. . . The reins of salvation—reigns, rains—*always* controlling us, like Plato's black and white horses in the *Phaedrus*.

Once upon a winter afternoon Peter wrote a parable:

Keeping in mind that, as Kafka says, Judgment Day is a summary court in perpetual session—imagine the following:

. . . He finds himself standing before a panel of three judges, one of whom keeps looking at his watch—Tee-time is nigh.

"You are allowed to judge yourself," another judge thunders.

Ecstatic, he chooses his words carefully. "Very well—I have lived an exemplary life, free of sin—no regrets!"

Tee-Time nods. "The sentence is passed."

"But what is the sentence?"

"That is the sentence."

Guess who Tee-Time is.

23.

The roses have gone bonkers.

Is it the wind? Is it my mood? Is it . . .

Peter (contemptuously?): *For you, buddy, a rose is not a rose is not a rose is not—*

Anyway, there're petals strewn everywhere, summoning up my grandmother's words of long ago: *Everything in its proper place.*

The gods do provide plenty of elbow-room for craziness. So why—

Never mind. Here's Don Paterson:

Wouldn't it be wonderful to start our children's spiritual education at the age of six with the honest opener: Children, I'm afraid no one has the first clue why we're here . . .

24.

One day I knew I'd return to the classics.

And so I have: re-reading Plutarch's *Nine Greek Lives.*

Among them: the wily and dangerous Themistocles, who said, "I cannot play the fiddle; but I can make a mighty state from a little city."

Well, maybe. Peter can't make a mighty state from a little city, but as I say he did play the triangle in second grade; pretty good at it, too.

I once dreamt of traveling through time, plopping down in the agora in ancient Athens dressed up in period costume, in full command of demotic Greek.

A group of learned men approached and politely asked me a number of questions, which I answered truthfully. I told them I was from the far future—which they accepted with equanimity!

Then I turned to the subject of myth—what we moderns dismiss as nonsense.

Proud of myself, I recounted their myths as the waterclock in the agora changed and changed again.

When I finished with my litany of Zeus, Athena, Poseidon, Apollo, etc., the Athenians stared at me blankly, uncomprehendingly, as if I were from another planet, never mind the future.

Peter: *I told you so.*

25.

The train rolls to a stop in the middle of nowhere and the lights go out.

"We've lost power," the conductor speaks into his walkie-talkie. "No telling—"

"I'll lose my ice," murmurs Suzie the bartender, and I knock down my second vodka and tonic in a hurry. Through the bar car windows I see fields of cotton rolling to the western hills of the San Joaquin Valley. The hills, too, are melting in the heat-haze.

I'm heading back to Berkeley from Hanford, where my girlfriend Kay and I broke up the night before.

In the middle of the journey of our life, I entered a dark wood—

Hardly! Still, as the temperature in the bar car starts to climb, I remember a voice waking me up in the motel room last night. Dreaming of endless rows of apple trees in my own valley, the Santa Clara where I grew up, a cry from boyhood awakens me:

"Steven!"

It's Peter.

I'm alone—Kay's family put me up in the motel—but I look around the room, even getting out of bed and checking the bathroom. Like now—but half-awake—I'm sweating.

And yet there was something—what?—*compelling* in Peter's voice: a secret sharer of my disappointment of the night before.

The power comes on, Suzie gets back to work, and I sit there, ice melted in my drink . . .

26.

Twirling lariats of stars—ghost riders in the sky, roaming the gods' eternal grasslands.   Or is it ghost writers?

The gods have gone AWOL.

What else is new? The best these spectral good old boys can hope for is a saloon and a brothel. . .

(Peter wrinkles his nose at this thought which, of course, amuses me no end).

. . . Three a.m.: I get up to pee. Before going back to bed I make my pilgrimage to the window, slide it open, and hear the insistent drumbeats of Respighi's *Pines of Rome*.

Ah, no. Make that the drum tattoo of a funeral procession consisting of my parents, grandparents, aunts and uncles—all marching blissfully, or so I hope, in the ranks of death.

Hope . . .

Because I'm writing this in north L.A. county Jack Spicer's words come to mind:

The three main residential streets of Los Angeles were named Faith, Hope and Charity. They re-named Faith and Charity but left Hope. You can sometimes see it still in the shimmering smog of unwillingness.

27.

There's an Arabic word which means *that which must not be seen*.

We close our eyes when we kiss. Why? Maybe because we're subliminally afraid to "see" the inamorata—see into his or her soul, I mean, the eyes being windows, as the saying goes.

I also like the Arab superstition about the camera eye; once upon a time they avoided cameras lest their souls be imprisoned forever. In Hollywood, of course, the opposite obtains. Robert Redford and Clint Eastwood could take a hint from the Arabs.

Every time the moon-goddess (Selene; Hecate; Mano; Luna; Chang-e) gazes down on me, I swear I hear a camera-click.

Eyes closed, Peter chirps: *Say cheese!*

Darkness
One
Embracing
Size
Us
Fits
Both
None

28.

Words—(s)words—are weapons of war.

Sometime all it takes is one measly letter added or subtracted and—

Change of word, change of sentence, change of worlds—

Imprisoned by words—sentenced, I mean to say, to a life-term: "in for all day," as my student-inmates at Arizona State Prison used to say.

We can always be friends. I'd rather she said *I hope you burn in hell.*

Appalled, Peter frowns at this—but I'm in deadly earnest.

As I pointed my '57 Plymouth north toward Berkeley, the Logos became the Low-ghost, as Jack Spicer puts it. So it remains, fifty years later.

. . . She stood there in the porch-light, hand on the doorknob but looking back at me:

I wish I had the words.

> The
> ***Now***
> Kisses
> ***Then***
> For
> ***Now***
> The
> ***Now***
> Love
> ***Then***

29.

Peter: *Good things come to those who wait.*
Steven: *—Bad things, too, man.*

. . . I've always loathed waiting—even in a dentist's waiting room for a root canal.

I've been stood up more than once; almost as bad as waiting are the mind-games you play with yourself:

Her car wouldn't start.
She's feeling ill.
A friend or relative dropped in unexpectedly.
Etc.

What happy horse-dung! Almost as bad: waiting for an email or for the phone to ring. Another game— reverse psychology: It's a marketing call; it's A, B, C, D, or E (a litany of friends); it's a wrong number; it can't be her.

Or—

Take a number and stand in line, please; your call is important to us: please wait for the next available representative; there will be a forty-five minute wait before we can seat you; so-and-so stepped out of his office for a moment; would you like to hold? Bridge construction ahead: expect delays of—

Etc.

And yet I have to admit that waiting is a, maybe the, perfect incarnation of spiritual obedience. Yes, we feel like victims, waiting helplessly for Necessity to lower the boom.

Peter quotes from Simone Weil:

On account of its perfect obedience, matter deserves to be loved by those who love its Master, in the same way as a needle, handled by the beloved wife he has lost, is cherished by a lover.

The beauty of the world gives us an intimation of its claim to a place in our heart. In the beauty of the world brute necessity becomes an object of love. What is more beautiful than the action of gravity on the fugitive folds of the sea-waves, or on the almost eternal folds of the mountains?

The sea is no less beautiful in our eyes because we know that ships are wrecked by it. On the contrary, this adds to its beauty. If it altered the movement of its waves to spare a boat, it would be a creature gifted with discernment and choice and not this fluid, perfectly obedient to every external pressure. It is this perfect obedience that constitutes the sea's beauty.

30.
(1946-1953)

My Baby Boomer childhood was punctuated by little deaths.

First to go was the field south of Alto, where we dug caves until the mothers showed up and collapsed them, telling us someone could smother. (I resented this, Peter did not).

No matter: something-or-other Manor, a cheap housing development, gobbled up the field.

Next: the hill south of town, across the highway. It was studded with beautiful live-oaks, including one with a rope swing someone's dad had attached to a sturdy limb. The trees gave way to Enchanted Knolls, a gated community looking down on Alto.

Next—but you see the point.

Then there were the real, un-metaphorical deaths, little in no way, shape or form.

I can still see her—Robin, a pretty eight-year-old with dark hair, wearing polished black leather shoes with straps, and white socks. One summer she simply disappeared, no one knew where until my mother told me she'd died of polio.

Tommy McCaffrey, the obnoxious kid next door, scion of a white-trash family, or so my mother called them, grew up with me until we moved to the San Francisco Peninsula, where I entered my first foster home.

Three or four years later, on a return visit to Marin County, we learned that Tommy had drowned when, on a speed-boating trip to a lake in northern California, his dad—I.Q. in negative numbers—let him ride on the bow without a lifejacket.

I "absorbed" these changes, not out of acceptance or resignation, but because I felt there was always something else quivering on the horizon (more deaths, it turned out).

A little child shall lead them—

31.

A few years ago I wrote a parable:

A man, who as a small boy had witnessed the death of his father, was reminiscing with Charlie Johnston, an old family friend now in his seventies.

"Do you remember," he asked the friend, "the time you took us neighborhood kids on a hike in the hills above Alto?"

"I do," the friend nodded. "Someone brought streamers made of red and gold crepe paper, and you children ran up and down the hills, trying to fly them like kites. But what I remember in particular was how angry you seemed; you kept using words I never thought I'd hear from a boy that age."

The man leaned forward—eagerly, or so it seemed to Charlie Johnston.

"And of course that was after my father died."

"No, no, before . . ."

"Before!" the man leapt to his feet; "my father was still alive?"

"Your father was still alive."

The man sat down, speechless; for he'd always assumed that his anger . . .

—Then, as Charlie Johnston gazed tactfully out the window, the man's mind clouded over; and he felt once again that strange rage toward the father, the father, that he died, leaving the boy and his doppelganger behind many years ago.

32.

Dear Mom:

—I compared memories of witnessing your death to an amethyst, your favorite stone: every facet etched by the clear colors of my precise recollections of that night.

The funeral, on the other hand, is a lump of jade: memories impenetrable: faint, muddy light obscuring everything.

(Peter and I agree on this: neither of us remembers a thing of the funeral.)

Now, as I flirt with age seventy jade, so to say, has gotten the upper hand, so that your ghostly appearances are less mnemonic than poetic: as if in death you've become, not an angel, not even a muse, but a Virgil, guiding Peter and I through the hell, the purgatory, and yes, the paradise of our souls.

33.

So fluent in a world of saguaro and ocotillo, tonight's desert moonlight has nothing to say to Peter and me.

—Starlight: equally incommunicado.

No matter. The wind picks up in the mesquites which resent being rousted from a sound sleep.

But the stars—the stars—

> The
> *Cold*
> Wind
> *Light*
> Has
> *From*
> No
> *A*
> Shape
> *Newborn*
> Save
> *Star*
> In
> *Still*
> What
> *On*
> Resists
> *Its*
> The
> *Merry*
> Wind
> *Way*

34.
(Two popular songs)

1.

Out where them chilly winds don't blow—

He means *west,* folks—west of the cold Colorado rain and his lady love.

The saddest songs—and John Stewart's *Chilly Winds* is right at the top—are the most beautiful. Why?

Never afraid to state the obvious, Peter says, "Because they're the truest."

Once upon a chilly December morning I myself wrote:

Two women are talking in whispers; one is weeping.

"Forget him," the other waves her hand. "You'll find someone else, I promise you!"

"Oh, I'm not weeping over him," the other wipes her eyes. "I'm weeping for that time in the far future when I'll have no cause to weep!"

Think of Bashō, heart breaking as he looks at a friend's back recede in the distance. Watching as airliners carrying friends lift into cloudy skies, Peter and I have experienced that pang.

—And imagined:

As Bashō gazes at his friend, a dejected April moon rises— bereft of everything, even the sadness of a tea-song.

> *Leaving in the springtime,*
> *Won't be back till fall;*
>   *If I can forget you,*
>   *I might not be back at all—*

2.

Baby Driver

They call me Baby Driver,
And once upon a pair of wheels
I hit the road and am gone ah!
What's my number?

I'm riding shotgun; Peter's behind the wheel.

There's no way I know where this present volume is taking me. If Peter knows, he's not saying.

On the other hand, if I had a map of Point A to Point B, why make the real journey? When I verbalize this, Peter asks if I've gone bonkers.

When I was a kid we, Peter and I, loved maps, probably because I assumed we would never go there—"there" being anywhere fifty miles in every direction from where I lived.

What is it Melville says about Ishmael's friend's island home?

It won't be found on any map. True places never are.

But now that I have traveled in many countries, the feeling persists:

The territory is not the map.

The poet in me (here things get complicated) resists that feeling.

So, as I say, when I sit down to write I struggle not to discover where I'm headed. –A task made easier thanks to the trusty glass of chardonnay at my elbow.

—All this, even though a favorite poem ends with:

Drive, he said,
For Christ's sake look where you're going—

      Colors
      All
      Touching
      Those
      The
      Lovely
      Lake
      Drinks

35.

The strangers sleeping within—all the mothers and fathers we're not aware of . . . Do they exist in my facial expression as I try to make sense of last night's bad dream of the great-grandfather who killed five people in a Kentucky family feud?

Or in my walk, which someone once compared to a sailor's rolling gait?

—Or in my laugh? (Peter rarely laughs.)

Sometimes—not always—Pete reminds me of that French statesman who boasted that in his entire life he had "never made ha-ha."

I'm as much a stranger to myself as the strangers are to me. That'll change when, years from now, something of Peter and me—something in us—shows up in the walk, talk, or smile of someone yet to inherit Paradise—for one or two winks of eternity.

Kids
I
In
Stroll
And
The
Out
Garden
Of
Of
The
Their

Rose
Eternal
Garden
Hours

36.

A feminine voice: *If dreams came true we wouldn't be living in truth but in dream.*

Or is that Peter's voice? Sometimes—

Caught in the warp and woof of sleeplessness and dreams of sleeplessness, I watch the moon, or dream-moon, rise in the west until it paints my walls silver-yellow.

I scribble in my note-pad, then put it back on the bedstand and turn off the light. Once my eyelids become heavy, I feel certain that the urgency to go there will return and, asleep, I *shall* go there—Palo Alto, where I lived off and on with my brother and mother until she moved up to Berkeley to die, then lie in repose next to my father in the cemetery at Saratoga.

Our 957-square foot home on Emerson Street was sold of course, so I don't know where to find her. Is she in an apartment, a rental home, or a resident's hotel like the one I lived in my senior year at UC Berkeley?

But she passed away more than forty years ago, Peter whispers in my ear.

I choose to walk northward over California's dark coastal hills, tossing Peter's remark in a clump of fennel bushes—yellow in sunshine, gray in darkness. In the east a pale moon refuses to turn her cheek and reveal the dark side, repository of all lost things.

It's two or three hours before dawn, but I know I won't arrive before noon, and something tells me by then she'll be gone. And the old selfish feeling returns—the feeling I had as a boy after my father's death, when I fretted away many nights about her dying—*What'll happen to me now?*

37.

Point—

We hate to admit that far from being an escape, day-dreaming is a form of exile.

Play the game of *What if,* and bingo! You're on the outside looking in: poor Ovid exiled amid the barbarians, dreaming of Rome; beard pointed south, Dante dreaming of Florence.

Taunting the poet of the Divine Comedy, the River Arno runs clear for once! And Beatrice, who married a butcher, never gets old.

Is it—is day-dreaming—in our DNA?

Peter: *I hope not.*

Not to say that day-dreams don't come true; it's just that they represent a desire to confront, even embrace, our secret desire for exile.

Why did Eve eat the apple? OK, Peter—spin in circles until you fall down: then repeat after me:

Hello? —Because she was bored.

Counterpoint—

The still waters of our longing for Paradise—the joy it provided and the grief of losing it—run shallow.

God help us, our longing for other things runs deeper.

Closer to home—I'm thinking of Swan Lake village—I enjoy the sound of Bond Creek flowing 100 feet east of the bar.

It's syncopated to Phil's bar-talk of his wife of twenty years who recently left him.

She had the perfect gig, he tells me, wiping the bar. Two wonderful kids, a good husband—I think I can say that—and a paradise to live in. I mean, how could Swan Lake be more beautiful?

Coda—

Apprehend means two things: To capture, and to "grasp," i.e. understand; cf. its kissing cousin, *Comprehend*.

It's a word I don't like to use when speaking of beauty.

Peter agrees: *Try apprehending beauty in words, thoughts and feelings; and poof! The thing of beauty disappears and you disappear.*

When we fall in love with beauty, tears are often conjured but never laughter. Why?

(I don't mean tears of joy. I mean something more profound.)

There's a nether-region somewhere (in the cortex?) beyond tears and laughter.

Peter surprises me: *In other words, tears are a substitute for something.*

Correct! We get a feeling for what this *something* is by watching Greek tragedy which rinses out the eyes, but not with tears.

38.

Both Peter and I balk at being referred to in the second person—that is, at referring to ourselves in the second person. This, too, makes us one. —But why?

Moon
The
In
Rain
Your
Knows
Glass
Only
Of
One
Chardonnay
Thing

39.

Where was I? Oh—Metaphor, too, is a form of exile.

We go from eyes (the tenor) to limpid pools (the vehicle) because there's another truth we don't care to face: namely the possibility that we are metaphors and the images of imagination are real.

Peter: *That's nonsense!*

Let's take a step back and catch our breath.

. . . So what's the tenor to *our* vehicle?

—Dreams, naturally! Not day-dreams: "real" dreams, performing a dance macabre for the insomniac moon.

Peter: *Oh, for—*

What if—

What if the moment of death is a vehicle spawned (a salmon up the river!) by the tenor of birth?

Or is it the reverse? I forget, not being dead yet.

Peter (shaking his head): *Steven, none of this adds up.*

Silence
1
After
+
The
1
Night-
=
Birds'
0
Cries

40.

Are there metaphors in Purgatory? In Hell?—

Without judgment, no forgiveness!

But, as Peter has written before: in Hell, no judgment therefore no forgiveness.

Peter: *Leave me out of this.*

Now—just now—I think I have an answer to the question.

In Hell *everything* is a vehicle: eyes, limpid pools, day-dreams and night-dreams.

And the girl with a lazy eye you meet at the bar; in Sartre's No Exit, the long blue hill to heaven no one bothers to climb; in Spain, the last #11 Palo bus from Malaga at two a.m.; the owl-clock you buy for no good reason at an antique store—

Peter (sighing): *Second person again!*

He's right; I forgot.

(But yes, there are owl-clocks in Hell—prompting (forgive me!) another question:

Which would you prefer in the Infernal Regions—clocks or clocks without hands?)

One exception to the rule of metaphor:

In hell, the words are real: tenors coming back to haunt you. I mean loving words you never uttered—

Peter: *Damn it all, what did I just say about the second person?*

      Whistling
      Fireflies
      Past
      And

The
Stars
Graveyard
Deepen
You
The
Hear
Darkness
Whistling

41.

Must Peter be sacrificed to the darker angels of my nature?

He laughs unexpectedly: *Not to worry! Remember DNA—*

On the other hand, he adds, *I have no intention of playing Jiminy Cricket to your Pinocchio. I mean, who talks about the superego anymore?*

So what are you good for? I'm tempted to ask.

(The mirror—thank Zeus!—has no reply.)

    Trembling
    Reflections
    For
    In
    Both
    The
    Of
    Pond
    Us

42.

Sometimes I (or is it Peter?) feel like an imposter. Sort of like those identical twins who switch places to see if girls can tell the difference—

"Sort of": because, of course, Peter and I aren't identical. *Thank God!* We chirp in unison.

I always think of Peter when I revisit a wonderful *New Yorker* cartoon from many years ago.

Two men are checking out a gravestone, which reads:
Here lies an officer and a gentleman.

"Strange," one man turns to the other. "I wonder how they came to be buried in the same grave."

        Dying
        Comedy
        Is
        Is
        Easy
        Hard

[The last words of the great English actor Edmund Kean]

Book III

Hic et Ille

Steven:

When it comes to sexuality, American women rarely arrive. When they're emotionally immature and their bodies are ripe, they don't know how to harmonize their inner and outer erotic existences. For instance, they'll flirt to attract a man sexually, but if the man says "You have a beautiful body," she balks—half-contemptuously, half in apprehension, chanting the old mantra to herself: *I don't want to be wanted for my body alone.* Thus sex with guys often results in shyness, embarrassment, even discomfort.

But when women—again, American women—are emotionally mature and the bloom on their bodies has faded, erotic balancing of their outer and inner lives usually isn't an option. Here, too, sex with husbands results in discomfort tinged, perhaps, with sorrow ("Well, I did my duty again last night," a frowning female bartender once confided in me).

(Affairs change the equation, of course, but they rarely last).

Bottom line: the inner and outer erotic lives of most American women are ships that pass in the morning and the evening of their lives.

American guys have it easier—or so it must seem to women. Erotically coarser than women, they perceive their bodies as mere tools—as separate from states of immaturity or maturity as hammers and saws are from the workmen who wield them.

Peter's response:

Booted out of the Garden, were you consoled, Steven, by

the pale purples of foxglove blossoms?

We'll miss you, the flowers murmured to me as a breeze sprang up.

I'll miss them too—except that I know that you, Steven, are on a mission to recapture the unholy grail of your youthful passions.

Still digesting the apple, where did Eve think she was headed?

Speaking of consolation, do you recall falling in love with Eve in Michelangelo's *The Expulsion from the Garden?*

OK, OK, she's... *Dumpy* is being charitable. Shamefully, this comforted you because unattractive females were never a threat to your ego.

If they wouldn't listen to reason, like a coward you could always tell yourself:

Oh, well, she wasn't that hot...

Whatever happened to tender feelings for women?

From the bare ruined choirs of Purgatory, voices of American women sing to both of us:

Tenderness, too, is dying on the vine in the Garden.

Peter:

Yes, yes, to doubt nothing and everything is the surest way of knowing nothing. The only equilibrium between these two poles of doubt is a) happiness or b) misery. So many choose misery!

Steven's response:

Keep in mind, Pete, what Sartre said of Camus—he never goes anywhere without a pulpit!

Steven:

"He who communicates an untruth is not made poorer by a lie." Given what Mr. Congreve calls the way of the world, dare we add—*No, he becomes richer!*

Peter's response:

The man who tells lies merely conceals the truth; the man who tells half-lies has forgotten where he put it.

Peter:

[Paraphrase of a *Syracuse Post-Standard* news item in 1989]:

In a 182-page book, an Italian shrink details the cases of 106 patients admitted to a Florence psychiatric hospital over a ten year period. They suffered from paranoia, disorientation, and delirium brought on by exposure to magnificent works of art. Hundreds of milder cases, probably thousands, have gone unreported . . . "The worst case had to be hospitalized ten days," reported the shrink, also a lecturer in psychiatry at the University of Florence.

Steven's response:

Ten days on a psych ward? I would've quoted Nietzsche to that worst case: *We have art that we may not perish from the truth.*
Problem solved!

Steven:

Like eggs on Easter morning, invisible gifts lie all around us.

Here's one: If given the opportunity to relive our lives—including the "good" parts—and if we thought long and hard and honestly—we'd instinctively recoil in horror. Once is enough—no, no, more than enough.

Peter's response:

If by the "good" parts you mean the successful parts, then my response is: Not only can you argue with success, you should argue with success—as with an adversary.

Peter:

Someone wrote, "I wonder if any animal looking at us thinks, 'Ecce Homo'?"

. . . We celebrate language as the great achievement of human genius. But if animals had language and intelligence as we conceive of it, what would they think and speak of us—their supposed "lords of the earth." Recall how we employ names of animals to refer to one another: usually but not always in negative terms—dirty dog, braying donkey, filthy jackal, wolf in sheep's clothing, snake-in-the-grass, etc.

On rarer occasions we invoke animals to praise—"He has the heart of a lion," "She's innocent as a lamb." Were they conscious of themselves, would animals project their behaviors, their inner lives, onto us as we do them? If they were human-like, of course they'd see themselves differently than we see them—no jackal would admit to being filthy, no snake would think of itself as sneaky, etc. What names, then, would they call us? Maybe a better word is "could," not "would."

. . . No doubt there're infinite ways to try to understand ourselves: including fanciful and useless perspectives like this one. All we can do is fall back on that brave and ancient injunction: *Know Thyself.*

P.S. A wolf whispers in my ear: *Shouldn't that be Icky Homo?*

Steven's response:

—Right: but which self?

Steven:

Radical shrinks like R.D. Laing talk about the normalcy of insanity and the insanity of normalcy. Uh-huh. I wonder how many patients he's taken home to meet the wife and kids—a normal thing to do in a normal world.

Peter's response:

On the other hand, remember working as a tech on the psych ward back in the 70's. A positive reinforcement system was set up, consisting of small colored pieces of paper representing different levels of acceptable behavior. If patients behaved extremely well—if they followed treatment protocols to a "t"—they were given red squares; if reasonably well, green squares; if so-so, blue squares.

Late one night on graveyard, a youngish male patient showed up at the nursing station, where head resident Dr. Jerry Smith and I were updating charts for the morning shift.

"Hello, Richard!" Jerry said with that false heartiness which rubbed me—and some of the patients—the wrong way. "What can we do you for?"

Richard said nothing, picking up a sphygmomanometer and turning it slowly in his hands, as if he'd never seen one before. Then he reached in his pocket and brought out the dozen or so red and green squares he received during the last few weeks. Then he threw the pieces high over Jerry's head. As they fluttered down like confetti, Richard walked out, saying over his shoulder, "I may be crazy, but I'm not stupid."

Peter:

I've always been taken with Nietzsche's "The thought of suicide has gotten many a man through the night."

Steven's response:

On the other hand, more men dread the advent of dawn than the kindness which is night.

Peter:

It amazes me how often the phrase *one size fits all* applies to things in general.

Steven's response:

Except for human existence itself, where the opposite applies.

Peter:

I've always felt that we can't really lose our innocence.

Steven's response:

No, but we can be—and are—lost by it.

Peter:

Don't you think we owe it to ourselves—

Steven's response:

Probably! —But at what rate of interest?

Steven:

The more accurate one tries to be in writing autobiography—yes, the more honest—the more one seems to become "the fiction of oneself." (Pardon the scare quotes.)

Peter's response:

". . ."

Peter:

"More people would be free if they could arrive at the consciousness of their freedom."

Steven's response:

I'd substitute "less" for "more." Remember Sartre's phrase, *condemned to freedom.*

Peter:

"People in whom reason and emotion balance each other out" are attractive, admirable—even lovable.

Steven's response:

—Or should that be, "cancel each other out"?

Peter's response to Steven's:

Then they'd be dead!

Steven:

That's what I mean, damn it. I don't know about "reason," but we love the dead because they don't make emotional demands on us.

Steven:

"The golden years aren't so golden," Janice's grandmother used to say. And the old saw, "Getting old isn't for sissies." And yet—a strange contradiction: the older we get, the more "real" life seems to be, as suffering, loss, and misfortune comprise the sharp edge of reality—what we're powerless to change or escape from.

But it's *also* true—at least for me—that the more waking hours we spend in the world, the more dream-like it becomes.

Peter's response:

Yes. "A man that is born falls into a dream like a man who falls into the sea."

[Peter's quote by Joseph Conrad, from *Lord Jim*]

Peter:

Kindness, charity, and love of one's neighbor—such things are crafts, not arts. There's but one true art in getting along with others: hiding one's natural egotism.

Steven's response:

Would you have anyone in mind?

Peter:

Once upon a visit to the bank I told a very rude assistant manager, "Now I know why Christ threw the moneylenders out of the temple." I'm still chagrined that I said that.

Steven's response:

I'm not. —Anyway, not to worry. That Christ gave the moneylenders the heave-ho doesn't make compound interest any less of a miracle.

Peter:

The greatest philosopher is yet to be born.

Steven's response:

True that. And when he does show up, he'll teach his acolytes, "Do neither as I say nor as I do."

Steven:

I have a theory. To keep things interesting, God welcomes in a bad-ass spiritual gate-crasher now and then.

Peter's response:

—That we can't know who the gate-crashers are, or will be, is Calvinism turned inside out like a sock.

Peter:

We stop envying others when we learn that they envy us.

Steven's response:

Yeah, but remember that envy is the sincerest form of self-flattery, not to say egoism. Deep down—deepest down—the envious whisper to themselves, *Please make him/her more like me!*

Peter:

Remember the reader who said awhile back, "Steven, I know exactly what you were trying to say!"

Steven's response:

Funny, I didn't.